GRINCHLAND

A CHRISTMAS ROM COM

ANNE-MARIE MEYER

Copyright © 2025 by Anne-Marie Meyer

All rights reserved.

No part of this book may be reproduced in any form or by any electronic or mechanical means, including information storage and retrieval systems, without written permission from the author, except for the use of brief quotations in a book review.
First Edition: 2025

www.authoranne-mariemeyer.com

ISBN: 978-1-963633-06-1

*For those who are truly Christmas-crazed.
Who might benefit from a little Christmas rehab,
this story is for you.*

ONE
CLARA

"Merry Christmas!" the street vendor shouted as he shoved a snow globe in my face.

Abbie hooked my arm with hers as she pivoted away, no doubt knowing exactly how I was going to react to this man. I allowed her to drag me a few steps away before I suddenly twisted and broke free. In one swift movement, I was back to the street vendor, who had turned his attention to the older couple pretending to talk to one another as they hurried past.

If Abbie thought she was going to keep me from stopping, she was kidding herself. "It's December," I sang out.

"Clara..." She sounded like a mother exasperated with her child.

I waggled my finger in her direction. "We have a deal. For the sake of our friendship, no Christmas talk. No Christmas decorations. And no Christmas music—which I think is just a crime—until December first." I shrugged. "Then all bets are off." I rubbed my hands together as I turned my attention back to the rows and rows of snow globes laid out in front of me.

I picked up one with two snow people ice skating on a picturesque pond. There was something about the elegance and beauty of the moment that had my body warming. Even though Abbie didn't understand my obsession with the holiday, *this* was why I loved Christmas the most. It was the feeling of home I experienced when I decorated a tree, ate Christmas cookies, or sang a carol for a smiling family.

It filled my bucket in a way that nothing else could.

"I'll take this one," I said as I handed the globe to the vendor.

"That's a very popular—"

"And this one." I reached out and picked up a snow globe that depicted three snow people standing around a tree. The biggest one—the dad—was holding the plug for the lights in its little twig hand.

"Really? Do you think that's wise with your"—Abbie leaned in—"job situation?"

I knew exactly what she was saying. My job situation wasn't even a situation. It was a nothing burger. My substitute teaching job had finished last week, and there wasn't a prospect in sight.

"Look at its little twiggy hand," I said in a baby voice, choosing to ignore what she'd said. Life was better when I focused on what was important, like Christmas decorations. I held it close to her face so she could see just how ridiculously cute this one was.

Abbie humored me by glancing down at it. "Oh," she said, her skepticism fading a bit. "That is cute."

"And this one!" I exclaimed as I held up a snow globe with a snow couple and a little snow dog. "There's a puppy in it." I handed it to the vendor along with the snow family around the tree. "I need these as well."

Abbie scoffed. "You don't need three snow globes."

I shrugged. "It's December."

"I know you keep saying that, but I don't think your tiny house can hold any more decorations. Last year, I couldn't find a place to set down my hot cocoa much less walk around."

I waved away her worry as I picked up a snow globe of two snow people sitting on the couch in front of a fire. I chuckled at the irony as I handed it over to be rung up. "There will always be room for one more."

Abbie was appalled—but not surprised—that I left with ten snow globes in hand. By the time I handed the vendor the ninth globe, he declared that I was now his season's best customer and gave me a tenth one for free. I tried to convince Abbie that I was basically saving money as we headed down the snow dusted sidewalk, but that wasn't a cookie she was willing to bite.

Instead, she just hooked her arm with mine and said,

"I'll never understand you, but if it makes you happy, then it makes me happy."

I smiled at my friend. We were different in so many ways, but we allowed each other to be our own kind of different. Abbie loved purses and shoes. While I didn't understand her need for so many—you only have two feet—I still went with her to store after store as she searched for the special pair. I knew, come December, she'd let me be the holliest, jolliest Christmas-loving person that I tried to hide the other eleven months of the year.

We spent the rest of the afternoon stopping at vendors so I could peruse their holiday assortments. We ate at the local sandwich shop, Freddie's Footlongs, where I sipped on peppermint-flavored hot chocolate while Abbie settled on a diet Coke with light ice. Our feet were aching as we climbed the stairs to my small house on Main Street. I'd inherited this place plus a borderline-hoarder collection of Christmas decorations when my grandmother passed away three years ago.

I spent every Christmas growing up with Grandma Dawn. I'd inherited her caramel-colored eyes, dirty blond hair, and love of everything that sparkled. We were ride-or-die Christmas fans, and this time of year made me miss her that much more. Dad was MIA after he left Mom and me on Christmas Eve when I was seven, and Mom spent more time in rehab than out of it.

Christmas with Grandma Dawn was the only

constant I had in my life, and my memories with her were the memories I would cherish forever.

I pushed open the front door—my shoulder hitting the obnoxiously large wreath I'd hung November first—and walked inside. I set my bags down in the entryway and was in the process of pulling off my boots when Abbie joined me. She kicked off the bits of snow on her shoes before turning to shut the door behind her.

"It smells good in here," she said as she held onto the nearby wall so she could slip her shoes off.

"I made sugar cookies this morning," I said. I was out of my fluffy red jacket and had turned to hang in on the hook behind me.

"But I came to get you at nine."

I glanced over my shoulder and shrugged. "And?"

Abbie's jacket was off now, and she stepped forward to hang it next to mine. "So...what? Did you wake up before dawn to bake cookies?"

I blinked a few times, waiting for her to answer her own question. This girl had been my friend since middle school. Did she really not just *know*?

When I didn't answer right away, Abbie looked over her shoulder at me and sighed. "Why do I even ask?"

I snorted. "Why do you?" I brushed off my hands and turned to my spoils that were sitting, still wrapped, in the shopping bags. I grabbed the handles and headed to the kitchen.

"I guess every Christmas I secretly hope that you will come to your senses and be normal..."

She'd stopped in the entryway and stared at the three trees I'd set up a few weeks ago. I may have promised my best friend that I wouldn't engage her in Christmas festivities outside of December. But here I could do whatever I wanted.

"Really? Three?"

I set the snow globes down on the counter and then walked back so I could catch her gaze. If I didn't act fast, Abbie would get trapped in the spiral of *"Really, Clara?"* followed up by *"Don't you think you're over doing it?"* and the pièce de résistance, *"This is not normal."* It was better to be proactive and help her move on from the shock of my house than to let her continue down this path.

"Come on, the cookies are cold now. We can decorate."

Abbie glanced over at me. I could see that she wanted to say something, but I just waved my hand in an effort to coax her into the kitchen. "I have almond-flavored icing," I sang out.

Abbie glared at me. "My weakness," she said as she made her way toward me.

I patted her on the shoulder as she passed by. "I know."

We were elbow-deep in spreading frosting on reindeer, Santas, and Christmas trees—well, *Abbie* was spreading. I took my cookie decorating seriously. I had multiple bags of icing laid out in front of me while I painstakingly took my time piping out every detail on Santa's face—when my phone rang.

My hands were sticky with sugar, so I did my best to find the one finger that wasn't coated to answer the call.

"Jingle, jingle, Clara speaking. Ready to *sleigh* the day?"

I heard Abbie snort. I shot her a glare before I turned back to my phone. That was exactly how Gran had answered the phone throughout December. Sure, it was a little corny, but sometimes people needed a little corny in their life.

"Um, hello?" the female voice on the other end of the call asked. "Clara?"

I slid the phone closer to me. "Yes, yes! This is she." Maybe that greeting was a bit too much. On numerous occasions, phonecalls had started in complete silence as if the caller had not been expecting it and needed a minute to catch up.

"Oh, good." Pause. "Anyways, this is Maria. Maria Thompson."

"Oh!" Memories came flooding back to me of my student teaching days with her as my mentor. "Hey!"

We chatted for a few minutes about what she was up to. Apparently, last year she'd taken a principal position at an elementary school. I was so happy for her even though my own teaching career was struggling.

I was excellent at finding long-term sub jobs, but none

of them had led to a full-time position. Teaching jobs were sparse in a small town like Winter Springs, Maine.

"I was calling because I'm in a little bit of a pickle."

I gathered some icing drops from the counter with the tip of my finger and then licked them off. "What's up?"

"My kindergarten teacher needs to go on an emergency sabbatical. I haven't been able to find someone who could come take her place with the holidays coming up. I was hoping..." She let her voice trail off.

I glanced over at Abbie, who was watching me with her eyebrows drawn together. As soon as my gaze met hers, she mouthed, *who is it?*

I ignored her question and shifted my attention back to the countertop. The thought of a job was appealing, but it was Christmas. The most magical time of the year. I couldn't imagine not spending it here, in Gran's house.

"I know it's the middle of the school year and last minute." She paused. "It does have the potential of being a full-time position."

My entire body froze. That was exactly what I wanted, no, needed. But Maria wasn't in Winter Springs. That meant I'd have to move to...I paused. What city did she say she lived in?

"How long do you need me for?" I asked as I leaned back and folded my right arm across my chest so I could rest my left elbow on my hand. It made it easier to hold my phone to my cheek.

"Just until the end of January, unless it moves to full-time. I need you here to close out the first semester. You don't even have to stay for Christmas break. All I ask is you be back by January fifth when school starts in the new year."

That was an interesting proposition. I could come back and spend the holidays here, in Gran's house, while still keeping a job. From the numbers in my bank account last time I checked, I needed something fast.

"There's a woman here that has a fully furnished place available to rent. I already talked to her about arranging for the new teacher to stay there since I knew I was going to need to hire an out-of-towner." She paused. "You'd really be helping me out of a bind."

Ugh. Maria was addressing every excuse I'd come up with for why I couldn't take this job. And I couldn't ignore the fact that I needed a job. I closed my eyes. "I'll do it," I said, excitement brewing in my stomach as I said the words. Then I frowned, trying to recall where the school was. "What city did you say you live in now?"

"Grinchland."

TWO
CLARA

"Ma'am, is this going?" One of the beefy men from Sexy Guys Move You lifted up my giant light-up Santa whose paint had faded from the sun and gave it a once-over. We were standing in front of my open garage door, and I was showing the three movers what was going to Grinchland and what was staying.

"Grandpa Santa? Um, yes sir," I said with a scoff. What a ridiculous question. "He goes with the reindeer ensemble. Without him, the whole sleigh and eight reindeer would look ridiculous." I waved to the items that another mover was currently trying to stack in the back of the moving truck.

Beefy mover glanced at me, then over to the truck, and then back to Grandpa Santa. "Um, sure," he said. The tone of his voice told me he didn't believe *that* would be the reason the ensemble would look ridiculous.

I wanted to explain to him why this Santa set meant so much to me—Gran and I found it on a trip back from Florida when I was fifteen, and we'd had to strap it to the top of her Volvo—but I already knew how these conversations went. I would get passionate, his eyes would go wide, his lips would slightly part, and just when I would take a breath to continue, he'd find a way to apologize and hurry away.

I'd learned that *I* may care about the history behind the decorations, but other people didn't. It was best to keep these stories to myself.

"Oh my gosh, Clara."

Abbie's voice drew my attention away from the movers as I turned to see her approach me. Her black winter coat was zipped to the top, and wrapped around her neck was the rainbow scarf that she'd bought on our trip to New York last year to celebrate her twenty-fifth birthday. Her cheeks were rosy and her eyebrows raised as she took in what we were doing.

"I thought you were coming home after school gets out," she said. She took a step back to get out of the way of the two movers carrying the giant nativity cutout that Gran had inherited from our church when they decided to go with a digital projector. Her gaze followed them as they made their way to the open truck.

"I am," I said as I glanced back and nodded to the beefy mover who had moved on to grab the cardboard boxes that were labeled *Outdoor Lights*. "But I'm not going to spend all December in a pathetically decorated house."

Linda, the landlord, had called me last night to give me the rundown. The house I was renting was a modest two-bedroom with one bathroom. It was fully furnished, just not "Pinterest furnished like you young people love." I almost told her that I lived in my grandmother's house, which hadn't been purged in twenty years but decided against it. Linda was chatty, and I had packing to do.

"You don't know it's pathetically decorated."

I scoffed and looked over my shoulder at her. "To me, it will be."

She sighed. "That's because you're *extra*."

"Am I extra? Or are others just basic?"

Abbie narrowed her eyes at me. "You're extra. Only extra people get a whole moving truck to move into a house that is fully furnished." She drew out the last two words. I watched as a thought dawned on her. "How are you even paying for this?"

I tsked her. "It's December," I sang out as I moved to grab the deflated dinosaur climbing a Christmas tree and headed to the truck. "The one month it's socially acceptable for me to be this obsessive, so I am going to milk it."

"You're crazy."

"You love me."

She paused and then sighed. "I think it's more that I'm stuck with you."

I handed the dinosaur up to the mover and then

turned to face Abbie. I grinned at her. "Soul sisters forever, no matter what."

She glanced at the line of movers carrying artificial Christmas trees who were passing by in front of her like a strange parade. "No matter what," she whispered.

She was starting to spiral, so once the movers had passed, I grabbed her hand and led her to the house.

"Come with me, I have some last-minute things to pack up."

After my car, the back of the moving truck, *and* the front of the moving truck were packed to the brim, I hugged Abbie, told her I would call her as soon as I got to the rental, and then climbed into my car, right next to Rudolf wearing sunglasses. The two-hour drive to Grinchland was peaceful. I was able to blare the Christmas music station as loud as I wanted without someone complaining.

Every town I passed through was fully decorated with lights down main street and the quintessential outdoor Christmas tree in the middle of town square. Which was expected. After all, this was Maine. Our state tree is an evergreen, and our state bird should be Santa.

When I saw the sign that said *Grinchland 10 miles*, I cheered.

I couldn't wait to see what they did for decorations and traditions. I secretly hoped their mayor would be open to some suggestions, 'cause I had a lot.

But as the mile markers began to count down, I frowned. Every house I passed was only lit up with plain outdoor lighting. No multicolored Christmas lights wrapped trees or roofs. There were no blowup figures. And not a single house had a decorated Christmas tree in the front window.

As the houses grew closer together, so did my confusion.

Nothing. There was literally nothing. Not a scrap of Christmas anywhere. If it weren't for the snow on the ground, I would have thought it was just another night. It was as if this town didn't know that it was Christmastime. *Did* they know it was Christmas?

Surely they did.

My phone's map app had me drive through Grinchland town square, where the people looked normal but the buildings did not. No lights. No decorations. No *tree*?

How could their town square not have a tree?

I blinked a few times and shook my head. Maybe they were just delayed. Maybe the town decorator was sick and hadn't been able to get started this year. It was a good thing I was here. Outside of work, I had all the time in the world. I'd spend my nights getting this town put together and shipshape.

But a sick town decorator didn't explain why no one was dressed in anything resembling a Christmas sweater or a Christmas scarf. It was just brown or black jackets and monotone accessories. The houses. The people. The atmosphere. It was like these people...didn't celebrate Christmas.

I shook my head in an effort to dispel that thought. There was no way, in the twenty-first century, this town didn't celebrate Christmas. There had to be an explanation for this. There just had to be.

Three minutes past town square was my rental. It was a cute house that sat back from the road. There wasn't a ton of yard space, but I'd make do with what I had. I pulled into the driveway and up to the small detached garage. There was a modest porch that wrapped all the way around the house. Even just looking at it, my mind was swirling with thoughts of how I was going to decorate it.

Maybe this town needed a little reminder of what this time of year was all about. I only wished Abbie were here —she'd be eating her words. If I hadn't brought half my decorations with me, I'd be stuck living in this lifeless city during the most magical time of the year.

I pulled open the driver's door and climbed out, the cool evening air whipping me in the face and causing me to inhale from the change in pressure. Once I was acclimated, I hurried around my car just as the movers backed into my driveway.

I stayed out of the way until they came to a stop, then I hurried across the driveway so I could locate the key— Linda said I'd find it hidden under the mat—and pushed open the door.

My lips pinched together as I glanced around. Modest wasn't the right word for this. Zero. Nada. Those were the right words to describe what I was seeing. Not a speck of Christmas anywhere. It was like the Grinch had sped up his timeline and stolen the heart of Christmas from this town.

I turned around and stared out at the houses that lined the street. I glanced over to my neighbor. The giant mansion sat in the middle of the property with an iron fence wrapping around the backyard.

Right now it looked ominous and overbearing, but give me a roll of Christmas lights and an inflatable penguin with a stocking hat and a giant candy cane, and this house would go from depressing to delightful.

In fact, this entire town needed a holiday facelift, and I was the exact person for the job.

THREE
SILAS

"...and I said if I had the power, Sheila, then I would. The mayor doesn't have the ability, so what makes you think that I do?"

Todd was still talking, but I wasn't paying attention anymore. First, Todd had this way of droning on and on about things I really didn't care about. Just because I was mayor didn't mean I needed to know every little detail about every little complaint that came in from the citizens of Grinchland.

The second reason my focus had shifted away from Todd was the sudden commotion going on outside of my home office window. A woman had pulled up to Linda Nexworthy's rental and was climbing out of her car. She looked younger than me, mid-twenties. Her long blonde hair had been picked up by the wind and was dancing around her head.

Sure, she was pretty, but that wasn't what had distracted me. It was the brightly colored red jacket she was wearing with a red, green, and yellow plaid Christmas scarf she had tied around her neck. Her gloves were the same pattern.

People didn't wear Christmas colors in Grinchland. Not since it was officially banned three years ago. To this town, December was just another month. Cold, dark, and depressing. The sudden appearance of this woman had me sitting up a little straighter as a sense of dread filled my chest.

"Mayor?"

A moving truck had now slowed in front of Linda's house and then started to slowly back up into the driveway.

"Silas?"

"Hmm?" I glanced over to see Todd was staring at me with a confused expression. He had his notebook out and his pen poised in anticipation of my response.

Todd paused. "Was there anything that you wanted me to specifically say to Mrs. Potts?"

I blinked at him, trying to recall what he had been talking about. Normally, I was always on the ball. I would look distracted, but when asked to repeat what had just been discussed, I could, with ninety-nine percent accuracy.

This was a first.

"Um..." Did I admit to Todd that I hadn't been listening? No, changing the subject seemed the better option. Plus, I knew I wasn't going to be able to focus until the sudden appearance of this mystery woman was solved. "Do you know if Linda Nexworthy rented out her house?"

I glanced back out my window to see that the woman and a mover were now standing at the back of the truck while the other mover unlatched the rollup door.

"Linda Nexworthy?" Todd paused. "The cashier at Shop 'n Save? I thought she had to go to Texas to help her daughter after her grandson's diagnosis. I didn't know she was renting her house out."

When I realized Todd wasn't going to be any help, I pushed off the armrests of my desk chair and slowly made my way to the window so I could peer down. The woman was now directing the movers who were removing all sorts of boxes and what looked like Christmas decorations from the truck.

I sighed as realization dawned on me. This woman was new. From the way she dressed and the obscene number of boxes labeled *Christmas Decorations*, I knew my peaceful December was looking a lot more grim.

Thankfully, most of the residents in Grinchland respected the decision we'd made as a town council when we changed the city charter to ban the decoration and celebration of Christmas. Most people who still wanted to celebrate left to do that elsewhere. Those who didn't mind, stayed. We'd even become a destination spot for people who wanted to avoid the holiday.

Some cities were *the* stop for all things holly jolly. We were the opposite.

"Who is that?"

I startled and turned to see that Todd was now standing next to me. Heat pricked the back of my neck. Todd was a fantastic assistant, but he was nosey. I stepped back from the window and settled back onto my chair, hoping that Todd would get the hint to drop it. "Get Linda on the phone. I need to ask her who is renting her house."

Todd lingered by the window for a few seconds longer as I shifted my focus to my computer and shook the mouse to wake it up. I wanted to know what the newcomer was doing now, but that was only going to fuel the flames of curiosity that I could feel building up inside of Todd.

Thankfully, he didn't linger by the window. Instead, he walked away while pulling his phone from his back pocket and typing away on the screen. Then, he handed it over to me.

Three rings and Linda answered. "Hello?"

"Linda?"

"Yes."

"It's Silas."

She paused. "What can I do for you, Mayor."

"Did you rent out your house?"

She let out a long, pointed sigh. "Yes, I did."

I pinched the bridge of my nose. "I thought we talked about you letting me know when you had a candidate."

"Well, since you've rejected the last five candidates, I

figured that no one was going to make you happy, and I need help with the mortgage. Maria needed a place for the new substitute teacher to stay, and she asked me if I'd rent her my house. Seemed like a win-win, so I said yes. Clara's a nice girl."

I knew that there was no legal way for me to fight Linda on this. We had a handshake agreement that I would let her use my parking spot at the community center if she promised to keep me in the loop when she was picking a renter. I guess our agreement was now null and void.

My lack of response must have had her scrambling, because she continued. "If it makes you feel better, she's just taking a substitute position. She'll only be here for a few months, and then we'll be right back where we were before." She paused. "I need money for gifts for my grandkids. I would appreciate it if you didn't scare her off."

I raised my eyebrows. "Scare her off?" I repeated. What did she mean by that?

"You can be...abrasive. Please let her stay there, keep the peace, and I promise I will let you pick the next one."

I didn't like what Linda was implying. Sure, I spoke my mind and I was forward, but what I said was the truth. It wasn't my problem if people couldn't handle it.

I cleared my throat as my gaze went back to the window. "Is she aware of Grinchland's holiday policies?" I already knew the answer based on the sheer amount of Christmas decorations currently being offloaded.

"I…um…" She paused. "I'll give her a call."

"You do that."

We said a quick goodbye, and then I hung up. I handed the phone back to Todd, who had been listening to our entire interaction. I could tell that he wanted to say something, but I ignored him, and Todd knew well enough to leave things alone.

Besides, Isabelle was going to be home from school soon, and I didn't like to mix work and family. I looked at the stack of complaints Todd had printed off. I leaned back in my desk chair and bounced a few times before I raised my gaze. "You asked me something about Mrs. Potts?"

FOUR
CLARA

As soon as the movers had finished unloading all of my decorations into the garage and part of the living room, I gave them a high five—which they cautiously reciprocated—and they drove off.

Now that I was alone, it felt only fitting that the first thing to do in the new place was to bake Christmas cookies. A sort of holiday christening. A way to get all the good juju flowing.

The smell of sugar and vanilla coated the rental as I pulled open the oven door with my Santa-shaped oven mitts. I took a moment to inhale the sweet, steam-filled air before I grabbed the cookie sheet and pulled it out. I was three dozen cookies in, and this never got old. There was something so soothing about cookies fresh from the oven, that it filled me with complete and utter calm.

Forget therapy, just bake Christmas cookies.

I chuckled to myself as I kicked the oven closed and then turned to set the hot cookie sheet on the hand-stitched pot holders of Santa's face that I made Gran in home economics in tenth grade. The fabric was worn in places, which only endeared them even more to me. It was a representation of the thousands of cookies that we'd made over the years.

My heart squeezed. I missed Gran so much, and I hoped I was doing her proud by keeping our love of Christmas alive.

I moved to pick up the reindeer-shaped spatula, and my phone buzzed, momentarily interrupting the Christmas music it was currently playing. I glanced down to see that it was a text from Linda.

> Just checking in to see if you're settled.

I smiled as I wiped my hands on my poinsettia patterned apron and picked up my phone.

> House is GREAT! So cozy. A little lacking in holiday decorations, but no worries, I brought my own.

After I sent the text, I watched as the three little dots started and stopped over and over again. I frowned. What was she trying to say? Finally, her text came through.

> I'm glad. Just stay away from Silas, the neighbor. He can be a bit grouchy.

I chuckled. "The Grinch of Grinchland?" I murmured as I started to respond to her text.

> I'll keep an eye out for vanishing Who-hash or disappearing Christmas trees.

Linda didn't respond, and the current Christmas song had finally started to amp up. I turned up the volume and began humming, but that quickly turned into singing and an impromptu dance party in the kitchen. My spatula became the microphone and my apron became the edge of my dress. I twirled and moved to the music. No one could ever accuse me of not immersing myself in the holiday spirit.

My cheeks were warm and I was slightly sweaty as the song wound down, so I leaned over and pulled open the nearby kitchen window. It faced the large, ominous mansion next to me. The place was dark and dingy during the day and even worse at night. It was in desperate need of some Christmas lights or an inflatable to brighten it up.

Just as I started to turn away, I paused when a shadow appeared in the top right window. It had the build of a man—Silas, maybe? The curtains were drawn, so I couldn't see details, just the outline. Then a smaller, more bouncy figure appeared next to him. Curiosity was eating me alive, so I leaned on my elbows to watch the scene unfold.

They were talking, the little girl and the man. He had his hands out like he was trying to get her to calm down—a stance I very much recognized from the last three years of teaching. The little girl settled as she turned so her back was to him. He looked like he was brushing her hair before it turned into some indiscernible movement that left me wondering if he was braiding it.

I smiled. That was sweet. Sure, they didn't have any Christmas decorations, which felt like a crime, especially with a child living there, but maybe they just didn't believe in Christmas. Too bad. Being with kids during this time of year was one of the reasons I became a kindergarten teacher.

Maybe I could introduce the family to the joys of this holiday season.

Realizing that I'd left the cookies on the sheet for too long, I turned and made my way back to the counter. I sang along with the music blaring from my phone but forced myself to focus on the task at hand. Maybe if I had enough cookies decorated, I'd bring over a plate to my new neighbors.

I was halfway through piping the outline for the Grinch cookies when three solid knocks sounded on the door. I frowned as I glanced around, wondering if I had heard right. When the sound didn't come again, I moved to start piping some more frosting, and the knocks returned.

There really was someone at my front door.

I set my icing bag down and rinsed my hands in the sink. I was drying them on my apron as I approached the front door. A dark shadow loomed in the narrow window to the side. If there were Christmas lights up, this person would have looked a lot less creepy.

I flipped on the porch light and unlocked the door. A man in a dark suit was standing there with his arms folded and a sour look on his face. He had dark brown hair and piercing blue eyes. His scowl could make even the happiest of gingerbread men frown. The only thing that looked excited to see me was the golden retriever sitting next to this man's leg with his head cocked to the side and an inquisitive look in his eyes.

"Can I help you?" I asked as I peered past him to the street to see if there was any clue as to who this man was and why he was here.

He did the same to me, glancing into the house before he returned his gaze to mine. "I'm Silas St. Nick."

My eyebrows went up. Did I just hear what I thought I heard? "Silas...St. Nick?" I asked. I couldn't believe my luck. What a perfect last name.

Silas's gaze darkened. "Yes. That is my name."

I nodded. "I love it," I whispered.

He frowned and peered down his nose at me like he was trying to figure out if I was joking. If he only knew how serious I was. Plus, I dealt with cranky five-year-olds all day. If he thought one sour look would have me cowering in my boots, he was sorely mistaken.

"What can I do for you, Silas *St. Nick*." I wiggled my eyebrows at him.

"What are you doing?" he asked, folding his arms across his chest.

I pointed to the ground. "Do you mean right now or before you knocked on my door?"

He paused like he was listening to something. "Are you listening to Christmas music?"

This was a strange conversation, but I was new, and Gran always said it was best to keep in the good graces of your neighbors. "Yep," I said with an enthusiastic nod. "And...I'm making *Christmas* cookies." I leaned in. "But don't tell the Christmas police." A light-hearted joke felt appropriate here. Hopefully, I could crack his icy exterior that even the most seasoned ice sculptor would struggle with.

Silas didn't even offer me a courtesy laugh. His lips remained flat and his eyes definitely weren't twinkling. He was not living up to his last name.

He sighed. Big. Like I was somehow inconveniencing him even though he was the one standing on my doorstep. "Since you're new, I'm going to let it slide and not cite you, but I would stop"—he circled his hand in front of me like I would know what he meant—"all of this."

Now I was super confused. I glanced down to where he'd motioned and then back up. "All of what?" I was trying to make one plus one equal two, but I was struggling to get there. Because the only conclusion I could come up with was so absurd that it hurt to think it. "Stop...Christmas?" I asked slowly, enunciating each syllable.

And then the most unthinkable thing happened. Silas nodded. *That's* what he meant?

"Yes. Participation in Christmas festivities is outlawed here in Grinchland. Hence the name. *Grinchland.*" He sounded it out as he leaned toward me and raised his eyebrows.

This was so insane, I laughed. This had to be a joke. Right? "You're joking."

But Silas didn't join in on my laughter. Instead he just stared at me. "I'm not joking."

I paused before I pointed my finger at him. "Was *that* a joke?"

"Good night," he said as he started to turn away.

My mind was reeling with questions, and I didn't want him to walk away before I could get any of them answered. "Are you saying that I can't celebrate Christmas? That I'm going to, what...get fined? Arrested?"

Silas didn't even bother to turn all the way around. Instead, he just glanced at me from over his shoulder. "That's exactly what I'm saying." Then he paused. "Except for the arrested part. But if you fail to pay the fines..." He shrugged. "It's up to you."

I sputtered as my brain short-circuited, trying to understand what he was saying. Silas, however, didn't seem to care. He glanced down at his dog and made a clicking noise.

"Come on, Dog," he said as he walked across the porch to the stairs.

Dog? He named his dog, *Dog*? How original.

"That's ridiculous. You know that, right?" was all I could manage to shout after him.

"I don't care," he called back as he continued down the walkway.

When it became apparent that he wasn't going to come back and tell me this was all a joke, some strange form of new-resident hazing, I humphed and hurried back inside. With the door shut behind me, I slumped against it. Was he serious? Was I really going to get *fined* if I tried to celebrate Christmas?

Was that legal?

The numbers in my bank account weren't going to support the amount of Christmas that just spilled out of me when I wasn't even trying. And it was December. The month I got to be...me.

I crossed my arms and stared at the floor. This had to be a joke. "You can't outlaw Christmas...right?" I whispered.

FIVE
SILAS

My morning alarm beeped right at 6 a.m. I flipped to my side and found my phone and silenced it. I was already awake.

Mornings were the worst. It was in the morning, when the house was quiet and dark, that I missed Nicole the most. We used to spend this time just her and I, shutting out the world. She'd get up and exercise before my alarm would go off. Then, when she'd come back into the room, she'd kiss me good morning before taking a shower.

Sometimes, I'd join her. Sometimes, I'd lounge in bed, enjoying the sight of my wife coming out of the bathroom, wet and wrapped in a towel. We'd make love or just talk as we got ready. Then we'd eat breakfast and head off to work.

I sighed as I stared up at the dark ceiling above me. My arms were flopped down by my sides. Most days, I managed to get myself up and out of bed before the wallowing could start. But for some reason, Nicole's memory was more poignant than it had been in months.

Maybe it had to do with Clara, Linda's new renter. Her zeal for Christmas reminded me of Nicole. She would look forward to December with a wonder and awe that I was a tad jealous of. The only thing in my life that came close to making me feel that way was...Nicole.

Three years later, the hole in my heart felt as big as on the night she passed away.

I pressed my fingertips into my eyes as I forced myself back to the present. I had a little girl who needed her father. I couldn't start spiraling now.

Needing a distraction, I pulled off my covers and padded over to the bathroom. I took a hot shower and quickly shaved. Once I was clean, I dressed in a black suit, styled my hair, and then headed out into the hallway.

Isabelle was already up and playing with her dolls on the floor of her room. She was still in her nightgown, and her hair was ratted on one side. The braid I'd put in last night, although lopsided, had managed to contain most of it while she slept. I wasn't a hair stylist by any means, but if it meant keeping the tears and the wailing down to a minimum the next day, I would attempt anything.

"Good morning, peanut," I said as I moved to join her on the floor.

Isabelle glanced up at me for only a moment before she returned her gaze to her dolls. They were facing each other, and it seemed as if they were deep in conversation about something serious from the way Isabelle kept her voice hushed and her eyebrows drawn together.

"Everything okay?" I asked as I dipped down to catch her attention.

"Shh, Jenny and Brooke are fighting," she whispered, not bothering to look up at me as she shifted one of the dolls side to side like it was talking.

Her voice was so soft, I couldn't quite make out what she was saying. So after a few minutes of observing, I decided to push her again. "What are they fighting about?"

Isabelle paused, her focus on the ground before she set both dolls to the side, drew her legs up to her chest, and rested her chin on her knees. "Catalina didn't invite me to her party," she said before she closed her eyes and jutted out her lip.

A protective surge rose up inside of me. "What? Why?"

Isabelle didn't speak right away. Instead, she just sat there in a clammed up little ball. I knew she was processing, and it was taking all of my strength not to pull her into my lap and hold her.

"Belly," I said as I tucked her hair behind her ear. "The princess can tell the dragon anything she wants."

A few weeks ago while reading Isabelle a story, she declared that I was *not* the prince but the dragon who guarded the princess. I didn't mind it. In fact, I loved the imagery it gave.

She sniffled as she lifted her head to look at me. "She just said that I couldn't come. It's at her grandma's house in some city." Her blinking grew more rapid, like she was trying to keep her tears from falling.

"Well, I bet it's going to be a boring party where they clean toilets and eat broccoli." She wrinkled her nose, and I matched it. "You don't really want to go do that, do you?"

She shook her head. "Blech."

I nodded. "Blech is right." I reached out and pulled her onto my lap, where I gave her a big squeeze. I was going to comfort my daughter now, but I had every intention of confronting Catalina's mother to ask why she was leaving my daughter out of this party. If she thought she was going to exclude my Isabelle, she had another thing coming.

"Do you know what you want to wear today?" I asked after I planted a big kiss on the top of her head, which she promptly tried to wipe off. "Hey!"

She ignored me as she climbed off my lap and stood. Her expression had changed from sadness to pure bliss. She had a plan and couldn't wait to show me.

"Wait here," she said, holding out her hands.

I pointed to the ground. "Right here?" I asked.

She giggled and nodded before turning to hurry to her closet. She shut the door behind her, and I waited. And waited.

Five minutes went by, and I was beginning to wonder if I'd lost her. I was about to call out to make sure everything was okay, when the door swung open and she came strutting out.

I tried to fight the smile that emerged. She was wearing a pair of neon blue, sparkly tights, an orange tutu with glitter polka dots, and a blue polka dot top with a giant rainbow scarf wrapped around her neck. And to top it off, she had a pair of Minnie Mouse ears that she got last year at Disneyland.

She twirled a few times, and I whooped and cheered. "You look beautiful," I said as I moved to stand. "Let's go wrangle your hair and eat some breakfast."

After her hair was braided into pigtails and her teeth were brushed, she led the way and I followed behind, shutting off the lights as I went. When we got to the kitchen, I declared it felt like a pancake kind of morning, so I got started pulling out the ingredients and setting them on the counter. I was adjusting the knob of the griddle when I heard Isabelle gasp.

Panicked, I searched the room only to find her by the sink, standing on her step stool. She'd risen up on to her tiptoes and was straining to see through the window.

In two steps, I was at her side. "What? What happened? Did you burn yourself?" I ran my gaze over her body in search of any indication that she was injured.

She glanced over at me, her bright green eyes as wide as saucers. "Look," she whispered as she shifted her gaze to the window and pointed.

I followed her gaze and my entire body froze. My

conversation with Clara last night apparently had *not* landed. Instead of heeding my warning, she was tromping through her snow-covered lawn with a giant reindeer in tow. But not only was she sticking reindeer in her front lawn, there was a Santa, a sleigh, and the largest, gaudiest nativity scene at the center of it all.

I blinked a few times out of hope that this was just a figment of my imagination. But every time my sight cleared, the Christmas decorations Clara was so defiantly staking into the ground were there to greet me.

Damn my 20/20 vision.

I sighed, frustration boiling up inside of me. If she wanted to make a good impression on the town she'd just moved into, this was not the way to do it.

"What is all of that?" Isabelle asked, her voice holding a sort of reverence that reminded me of Nicole.

"It's nothing." I wrapped my arm around Isabelle's middle and hauled her down. "Just our new neighbor being naughty," I muttered under my breath and then squeezed my eyes shut. Less than twenty-four hours since this Christmas-crazed woman had entered my life, and I was already using Christmas puns.

"It's so pretty," Isabelle said as she scrambled to climb up her step stool again.

"Aren't you going to help me make pancakes?" I asked, hoping to distract her.

"But—"

"I can't do it on my own." I gave her my biggest pout.

Isabelle studied me. I could see the desire to go back to the window fight against her desire to help me. Finally, she sighed and nodded. "Okay."

Luckily, I kept her sufficiently engaged in conversation about *Bluey*, her new favorite TV obsession, while we mixed, poured, and flipped the pancakes. And she seemed to forget the decorations.

I kept her away from the windows as I led her over to the foyer to get her shoes on. I stuffed her lunchbox into her backpack while she slipped on her coat. Once she was situated, we headed out into the garage and climbed into my truck.

I'd hoped that she would have forgotten enough to keep her attention on me and not Clara's house, but that was a pipe dream. Her face was basically plastered to the car window as we pulled out of the driveway.

I glared at Clara, who was in the process of climbing into her car and had paused to look over her shoulder. Her gaze met mine, and a defiant little twitch to her chin told me she knew exactly what she was doing. Heat pricked my skin as I pulled out onto the street and took a left.

On my way to the primary school, I called Todd. He answered in one ring.

"Hey, boss," he said, his voice breathy like he'd run to the phone.

"I'm dropping off Isabelle at school, and then I'll need you to go to my house. There's a citation to be written."

Todd paused. "You want me to write you a citation?"

I sighed. "You'll see when you get there."

Thankfully, there was a parking spot available right in front of the school, so I took advantage of it. Isabelle climbed out of her seat as I slammed my door. I rounded the truck and waited for her to grab my hand, and then we hurried across to the sidewalk.

Isabelle promptly dropped my hand as soon as we were inside the front doors. I followed behind her as she hurried down the hall to her classroom. Just as she neared the doors, she stopped and turned.

"Thanks, Daddy. You can go now," she said as she reached up to tug her backpack from my shoulder.

"Don't you want me to walk you inside?" I asked as I turned so she could get a good hold of her backpack, which I then let slide off my shoulder.

"No. I can do it myself." She walked over to her locker and opened the door. Once her coat was off and her backpack hung, she slammed the door. "No one else's parents walk them to the classroom. Only *you*."

The way she said *you* had me raising my eyebrows. If she picked up on my reaction, she didn't acknowledge it. Instead she threw her arms around my waist and squeezed. Just as I moved in to return the hug, she let go and headed to her classroom door.

"Bye, daddy," she called over her shoulder as she disappeared.

Now alone, I stared at the space she'd occupied just moments ago. Part of me wanted to walk in and demand that she let me drop her off. The other part of me—the part that won out—was happy she was becoming such a strong, independent girl. After Nicole died, I was worried that Isabelle would remember what happened. I worried that flashbacks would suddenly surface and she'd have to face the worst night of our little family's life all over again.

There was so much I wished I could change about that night—but I couldn't. I worried that I coddled her too much. That she would suffocate under my wing. But then I'd see her like this. Strong and independent. And it would only solidify that what I was doing was right.

There was nothing I wouldn't do to protect my little girl.

I sighed and turned, my fingers brushing her locker as I walked by. Just as I neared the office, I stopped. Normally, I would just wave to Pamela, the receptionist, as I walked past. But the sight of Clara had my entire body going numb.

That's right. She was here in Grinchland as a substitute teacher. How could I have forgotten?

There was no way I could just walk past and not say something. Especially to Maria. Clara may not care about the laws in Grinchland, but the principal was required to uphold them.

I could feel Clara's glare on me as I pulled open the office door and walked inside.

"Morning, Mayor," Pamela said her normal greeting to me.

"Morning, Pamela."

Clara scoffed. "Of course you're the mayor," she muttered.

I chose to be the bigger person and ignore her. "Maria available?" I asked as I made my way to her shut office door. I didn't wait for Pamela's response. As I entered, Maria looked startled before she quickly told whomever she was on the phone with that she'd have to call them back.

I closed her door behind me and then dropped onto the armchair across from her desk. I paused and steepled my fingers before I said, "Let's make sure we understand the rules, one more time."

SIX
CLARA

I could count on one hand—really one finger—the number of people I hated. Like, truly, deep-in-my-gut hated. Silas St. Nick was on track to bump that person from my list and become the *only* person I hated. I'd only known the man for less than twenty-four hours, and I loathed him.

And the fact that he was the mayor... "The mayor?" I whispered under my breath, still trying to process that new tidbit.

Pamela must have heard my question because she turned her attention to me. She asked, "Have you met Silas?"

I forced a smile and nodded. "Yes, I have met Silas. In fact, I'm his neighbor."

Pamela's face was deadpan as her gaze flicked down to the Christmas sweater I'd chosen to wear today.

In terms of Christmas sweaters, this one was understated. I even paired it with my green slacks as a sort of muted accessory. I had much more ostentatious outfits. Now that I'd seen Silas twice this morning, I wished I'd gone with one of them. It would have made my morning to see his eyes bug out ever so slightly over a *Christmas dress*.

Geez, that man needed to get a life if he let a little red and green bother him that much.

Before I could ask Pamela what the deal was with this town, Maria's door opened.

"Yes, Silas, I understand," she said as she stepped out of her office and off to the side so Silas could follow after her.

They shook hands and then Silas turned, his gaze sweeping over me for a moment before he walked out of the office. The air felt lighter once the door swung shut behind him. Maria puffed her cheeks as she slowly blew her breath out. Her gaze landed on mine and she raised her eyebrows.

"Hey, Clara," she said, her voice soft and inviting. It was just what I'd been looking for ever since I'd driven into Grinchland. Something familiar. Something welcoming.

"Hey, Maria," I said as I stood and hurried over to give her a hug.

Thankfully, she was still the hugger I remembered her to be. She didn't hesitate to pull me in and give me a big squeeze.

"How are you getting along in Grinchland?" she asked as she let me go and extended her hand toward her office.

I blew my breath out extra loud so she'd pick up on my exasperation. "Well, I thought it was going well until the *mayor* threatened to fine me for playing Christmas music in my kitchen." We were standing in her office now with the door shut.

Apparently, just talking about Silas St. Nothing—that man didn't deserve a last name that good—was a no-no. A worried look came across Maria's face as she glanced around like hidden cameras were everywhere.

"So I'm not crazy," I said as I plopped down on the armchair. "Your mayor is off his sleigh." I smiled at my pun.

Maria must have felt it was safe because she rounded her desk and sat down. "Silas is...interesting," she said as she grabbed a stack of paper from the sorter in front of her and tapped them on the desk a few times before she handed them over to me. "This is your HR pack. Let me know if you have any questions."

I took them from her, but instead of flipping through them, I set them on my lap. "Is that legal?"

Maria frowned. "What?"

"Banning Christmas? Like, this is America, right? There has to be some sort of freedom he's infringing on." I wished I had actually paid attention during my college history classes.

"Clara..."

"What does the sheriff think? Has anyone tried to fight this in the courts?"

"Clara..."

I glanced up to see that she was leaning on her elbows and studying me. She had the same sympathetic expression that I remembered from my student teaching days when one of her students would start to spiral because they couldn't draw a Thanksgiving turkey correctly.

Great. She was using kid gloves with me. I sat back and folded my arms.

"Grinchland is just that, *grinch* land. The town council signed the bylaws. There's not a lot we can do about it, so we've just accepted it." She shrugged. "I don't mind it. I'm not gaining holiday weight or overworking myself to decorate and entertain. I leave in the middle of December after school gets out, and when I get back, I have nothing to put away." She sighed. "It's not that bad."

I blinked. Once. Twice. Three times.

Grinchland was in America, but it was like she was speaking a foreign language. I understood the words she was saying individually, but the way she was linking them together created concepts that were alien to me.

"Canceling Christmas is *not that bad?*" I used air quotes to repeat her words back to her, hoping if she heard them, she'd realize how ridiculous they were. "I have daily traditions to uphold. What am I going to do about that?"

My chest squeezed, making it hard to breathe. What world was I living in? Was this hell? It felt like hell.

"I think you'll be okay." Maria offered me a consolatory smile.

She had no idea what she was saying.

I tapped my foot on the ground as my mind started reeling. I was not going to be okay. If I didn't have Christmas, then who was I? There had to be a way of changing these ridiculous Grinchland laws. I mean, I'm sure it would never become *Christmasland*, but there had to be a middle ground where everyone could be happy.

"Maybe Silas just needs to grow his heart a little," I said, more to myself then to Maria. "Maybe he needs to rekindle his love of the holiday." I glanced up and met her gaze. "Like Scrooge in *A Christmas Carol*!"

"Clara, I don't think that's a good idea. Silas is serious about this. If you step out of line, he's going to fine you."

I waved away her worry. "Once he's fully immersed in my holiday antics, he'll waive all the fines." I shrugged. "It's worth the risk."

Maria sighed. "I'm going to stay out of it. All I ask is that you don't rope the school into anything."

"Sure," I lied. I didn't have any immediate plans to involve them, but I liked to keep my options open. I was going to have to pull out my big guns to fix this one. My eyes widened as a hush fell over me. It was like I was Rudolph. Christmas this year depended on me.

"Let's go meet your class," Maria said as she moved to stand.

I nodded, plans still rolling around in my head as she

led me through the office and down the depressing and barren hallway. The walls weren't decorated with paper Christmas trees and finger-painted ornaments. There were no paper snowflakes hanging from the ceiling with countdown paper chains strung between them.

"What do the kids here even count down to?" I whispered under my breath.

If Maria heard me, she didn't respond. She stopped in front of a very plain door with a small window to the right. "Ready to meet your class?" she asked.

A spark of excitement mixed with nerves lit in my stomach. I loved and missed teaching, and it was always an emotional roller coaster to start somewhere new. I took a deep breath and then slowly blew it out. I was ready for some normalcy. My first impression of Grinchland had been so strange. I was ready to fall back on what I knew—teaching.

I gave her a big smile. "You betcha."

Maria pulled open the door, and I could hear the normal five-year-old chatter from where I stood. Nerves turned to excitement as she led me into the room. The voices quickly hushed as we stood in the center next to the whiteboard, facing the kids. Curious eyes peered up at us.

"Thank you, Mr. O'Brien," Maria said, and the man sitting behind the desk nodded and stood. He gave me a quick smile as he walked past, and once he was out in the hall, he shut the door behind him. I turned back to the kids as Maria took a step away from me and waved her hand in my direction.

"This is Ms. Snow. She's taking over for Mrs. Helen. She's going to be your teacher for the next few months."

I smiled as I swept my gaze around the room. Most of the kids didn't seem phased. They looked bored and antsy. There was a little girl with braided pigtails and a blue polka dot shirt who was staring at me. She looked worried, so I offered an encouraging smile.

"Thanks, Mrs. Thompson. I'm so excited to be here and to be your substitute teacher." I clapped my hands. "I know we're going to have so much fun and I'm going to be able to tell Mrs. Helen"—I glanced over at Maria to make sure that I heard her right; she nodded—"what an amazing class she has and how welcoming you guys were to me."

Maria's smile was encouraging as she glanced at the class.

The flow was starting, and I could feel the excitement of being in a classroom surge through me. I could do this. I could do this and *rock* at it.

"Why don't we go around the room and you can tell me your name and your favorite Christm—" I pinched my lips together to stop the words *Christmas celebration* from flowing out. My cheeks heated as I turned to Maria, whose eyes were wide as she stared at me.

This was going to be harder than I thought.

"What I meant to say was, your favorite color and why," I said, hoping the kids hadn't picked up on my blunder. "I'll go first so you can see what I mean." I cleared my throat and straightened. "Hi, I'm Ms. Snow and my favorite color is green. It's my favorite because it's the color of a Christm—" I pinched my lips together, halting the word.

What was wrong with me? I was going to leave Grinchland destitute if I couldn't put a cap on my love of Christmas. It was in everything I did—everything I talked about. This was proof that Christmas was such a part of me that I didn't know who I was without it.

All eyes were still on me, and I realized that I'd just stopped talking. So I offered them a wide smile and refocused. "It's the color of grass," I said, wincing at the reason. I loved green so much because everything Christmas started around the Christmas tree. The ornaments, the lights, the camaraderie that took place between the people decorating. If you didn't have a Christmas tree, was it Christmas? *That* was why I loved the color. I hated the mayor for forbidding me from speaking those words.

Grinchland and Mayor St. Kill-joy could just jump in a frozen, winter lake.

Listening to the little kids stand up and say their name and then their favorite color helped alleviate my frustration. Some voices were small and shy while others were large and boisterous. The mixture of personalities was the same in every class, and Grinchland was no exception.

When it got to the little girl with braids, she twirled her hair around her finger as she stood. "Isabelle St. Nick, and my favorite color is pink." She paused and I could tell that she was thinking hard. "Because I like bubble gum," she said with a wide smile that emphasized her missing front tooth.

St. Nick? Was that the little girl I saw in the window last night? I glanced back at Maria. "The mayor's daughter?" I mouthed.

She nodded. I stepped closer to her because I had questions. Isaac Parkes went on to introduce himself, but I was only half listening.

"That's the mayor's daughter?" I asked in a hushed voice while keeping my attention forward as Isaac sat down and the little girl with a dark bob cut stood.

"Yes," Maria whispered as she nodded at Melanie, who finished explaining in detail why aquamarine was her favorite color.

"Her mom is fine with not celebrating Christmas?" There was a reason Scrooge was a man, not a woman. They were the sex most willing to cancel the holiday. Silas was proof of that theory.

Maria paused, and I looked over at her to see if I'd missed her explanation. She met my gaze before turning it back to the kids.

"Her mom passed away three years ago when Isabelle was two." She nodded. "Thank you, Trudy. Orange is such a pretty color."

My stomach dropped as my gaze snapped over to Isabelle, who was doodling in a notebook while swinging her feet. While I didn't know that particular kind of loss, my heart ached for that little girl.

And maybe my heart ached a bit for Silas. Just a little bit. Or at least I was beginning to understand why he was the way he was. I understood anger. I understood grief. I understood wanting to lock the door and push the entire world away.

But canceling Christmas? Refusing to participate in the holliest, jolliest time of the year? That I didn't understand.

Christmastime was the perfect antidote to sadness. How could anyone feel bad when looking at twinkling Christmas lights or basking in the excitement of prepping for Santa? Maybe that was what Silas needed. A reminder of what made this time of year the best.

I'd decided to forgive Silas while I walked out to my car after school. Maybe we had just got off on the wrong foot. There were things about him that I didn't know, and vice versa. Gran had always taught me that there were always two sides to every story. And while I'd like to believe that Silas was the Grinch of Grinchland, life wasn't always so cut and dry.

I was going to go home, carefully wrap up the cookies that I decorated yesterday, and walk over to start fresh with the mayor. It was time to put the past behind us and move forward.

I saw a flash of gold run across my driveway, causing

me to slam on my brakes. It shimmied through the iron bars of Silas's fence.

"Dog," I muttered under my breath. I'd seen him come over a few times. I always waited to see if he was going to do something to my decorations, but he just trotted around and then eventually left. He was someone from that house that I actually looked forward to seeing.

I lingered in my driveway, just in case he decided to come back. I didn't want to accidentally hit him. But when it became clear that he was gone for good, I pulled forward and parked in front of the garage before turning off the engine. I grabbed my purse and teacher bag and pulled open the driver's door.

The cold winter air hit me and the snow beneath my shoes crunched as I climbed out of my car. I slammed my door shut then gripped the top of my zipper tighter to my chest as I hurried to my front door. I slipped the key into the lock, and just as my fingers grabbed the handle, I froze.

Right in front of my face was a white piece of paper taped to my door. Big bold letters at the top said, "CITATION: City of Grinchland." I scrolled to the neatly written reason above the word *offense*.

Public nuisance: Excessive storage of materials visible from the public right-of-way

I blinked. Excessive storage of materials? I glanced behind me. Was he talking about my Christmas decorations that I'd just started putting up this morning? And then I read a bit further down.

Total fee if paid within 21 days: $120.00

Heat pricked at my neck. One hundred and twenty dollars? Was he nuts? I sputtered. Why did it cost so much? All I wanted to do was share a little holiday spirit with the town. I pinched my lips together and narrowed my eyes.

This man...*this man*...

I wanted to think some thoughts that would definitely stick me at number one on the naughty list, but I had a better idea. He could write me citations all he wanted, but that was the coward's way of doing things. I would take the high road.

Ten minutes later, I pulled my front door shut behind me. Balanced on my right hand was a plate of perfectly decorated Christmas cookies. I'd wrapped them in cellophane and even used my good Christmas ribbon to tie it shut.

With the citation tucked into my jacket pocket, I rounded the fence, walked across his lawn, and up to the front door. A large, lion's head knocker sat in the middle of the ornate, wood door. I lifted it and let it fall a few times. Then I slipped my right hand under the plate of cookies to join my left and waited.

A few seconds later, the door opened and Isabelle's wide eyes stared up at me. "Ms. Snow?"

I smiled and leaned in. "Is your daddy home?"

SEVEN
SILAS

The oven beeped and the air smelled of basil and warm tomato sauce. I pressed the off button and slipped on the oven mitts that I'd pulled out of the drawer and set by the stove.

"It's dinner time," I called out to Isabelle. Last I'd seen her, she was twirling in the front room to a sing-a-long version of a princess movie that I couldn't name—they all blended together.

I set the steaming lasagna down on a pair of grey potholders and then slid off the oven mitts, stacked them on top of each other, and placed them back into the drawer where they belonged.

I heard the flap of the dog door that led into the mudroom off the kitchen, and I glanced over to see Dog scurry by. He kept his body pressed to the wall like he'd been doing something he shouldn't have and didn't want to get caught.

I thought about calling him back and confronting him, but my stomach growled. I was starving and ready to eat.

"Peanut!" I called out again, but the only response I got was the sound of someone knocking on the front door.

I wiped my hands on the dish towel hanging from the oven door before I went to answer it. I'd only taken two steps when I heard the door open and Isabelle's voice carry down the hall. I didn't like it when she answered the door before I knew who was there.

"Ms. Snow?" she asked. Her soft voice had a hint of reverence to it.

My body froze. Ugh. This wasn't going to be good.

"Is your daddy home?"

Shit. This was not how I wanted to spend the evening, although I shouldn't be surprised. I did have Todd leave a citation for her earlier today. I took in a deep breath as I walked out into the hallway that led from the kitchen to the foyer. I'd made a stand, and now I needed to own it.

Clara was standing in the doorway, holding a plate. Her cheeks were bright pink, and she looked flustered as her gaze moved from Isabelle up to me. For a moment, I saw anger flash in her eyes before it disappeared and she was smiling again—a bit too big.

"Hello, Mayor."

My lip twitched as I fought the smile that wanted to

emerge. Was it wrong that I liked the snippy way she said my title? I knew she was trying to be pointed, but it just came across as cute. Especially when she looked so disgruntled.

That was a strange, unwanted thought. I shook my head and cleared my throat, forcing myself back to reality. I needed to never, *ever* think those words again.

"Ms. Snow," I said as I nodded to her. When I got to Isabelle, I squatted down in front of her. "Peanut, what has Daddy said about you answering the door when a stranger knocks?"

Isabelle frowned. "It's not a stranger, it's Ms. Snow." She leaned in. "She's my new teacher."

My stomach dropped. Right. Clara was the new substitute teacher, I just hadn't realized it was for Isabelle's class. This was going to be a disaster. I glanced over at Clara. She had a soft smile for Isabelle, but when she shifted her gaze to meet mine, her smile turned forced.

I tousled Isabelle's hair, and she promptly swatted my hand away. "Go set the table, love. Looks like Ms. Snow wants to talk to me."

I could see Isabelle's whine start to build, so I reached out to touch her hair once more, and she sprinted away. Score. Worked every time. Now alone with Clara, I turned to face her. "What can I do for you, Ms. Snow?" I asked as I folded my arms across my chest and peered down at her.

She was staring straight ahead, her expression focused

like she was trying to gather her courage. The determination in her gaze was almost endearing. I valued people who stood up for what they believed in—even if what they believed in was a holiday celebrating overconsumption.

"I baked cookies last night. Thought I'd do the neighborly thing and bring you a plate." She held up the cellophane-wrapped plate. When I didn't take it right away, she continued. "I decorated them myself." Pause. "I've won multiple awards."

I kept my arms folded as I stared down at the cookies. I wanted to take them. My upbringing taught me it was rude to reject a gift, but the other part of me, the part that knew why she was here, refused. She wanted me to crack, but I was as determined and defiant as she was.

These were Christmas cookies, and I'd specifically told her yesterday that Christmas was canceled in Grinchland. It would be hypocritical of me to accept them. Any other cookies, and I'd happily take them. In fact, my stomach was yelling at me. But I remained steadfast, standing there with my arms folded.

"Are you seriously..." She paused and then blew out her breath. "Wow. Never in my life..." Her voice trailed off.

I leaned closer so I could stare down at her. "What did you say?"

She met my gaze and then shook her head. "Nothing. Never mind." She shifted the plate in her hands so she could pull out a folded piece of paper from her jacket pocket. "Care to explain this to me?" She made an attempt to unfold the paper with one hand. After a bit of maneuvering, she was able to shake it open and hold it out for me to see.

Yep, that's what I figured. She was here because of the citation. I shrugged. "It's a citation."

The look she gave me in response was one of pure annoyance. "I thought you were joking."

I frowned. I rarely joked, and even when I did, I would never joke about a citation. "I thought I made it pretty clear last night that you will be fined if you break the law." I flicked my gaze down at her with her red jacket and Christmas-patterned scarf. "The atrocities that you put up in your yard *knowingly*"—I emphasized that word so she knew I knew what she was doing—"clearly break the law here in Grinchland." I shrugged. "I would do the same with any resident here. You're no different."

She furrowed her brow. "But it says, excessive storage of materials." She looked up at me.

I nodded. "Your front yard is not a dumping ground for your stuff."

Her eyes widened. "Dumping ground...my stuff..." Her face turned red. "They're Christmas decorations. They're supposed to go on my lawn. They're supposed to be"—she paused and glanced down at the paper—"visible from the public right-of-way." She met my gaze. "What is wrong with you? What's wrong with this town?"

I took a step closer to her. I didn't appreciate what she

was saying. "Maybe there's nothing wrong with *us*. Maybe, it's you." I stared down at her. "Grinchland has been enjoying peace and quiet since the laws were put in place. No one's complained. We didn't stop Christmas for the whole world. If you want to celebrate, maybe go back to whatever town you came from."

She blinked once. Twice. Three times. I could tell that she was trying to think of something to say, but then she just sighed and took a step back. "So you're just banning Christmas. You can do that." The way she said the last sentence was almost like she was confirming with herself that it was true.

I shrugged. "Looks like it."

She glanced at the citation, then down to the cookies, then straight ahead toward my staircase that led up to the second floor. "What a waste," she whispered before she turned and twisted the door handle.

Once she was down my front steps and making her way over to her house, I shut the door and sighed. That's not how I'd wanted this evening to go. I didn't want to fight with my neighbor. Why did she have to be so stubborn? We had rules here for a reason, and even if she didn't like them, that wasn't an excuse for her not to follow them.

I hoped now she'd realize that I was serious and just fall in line. It would make things so much easier for me—and the town. In three weeks, Christmas was going to be over and this would all be in the past.

I flipped the lock on the deadbolt and headed into the kitchen. Isabelle had set the table with two mismatched plates, a set of utensils, a glass cup for me, and a plastic princess cup for her. The lasagna was cooled to an edible temperature, so I glanced around, looking for Isabelle.

"Peanut?" I called out as I grabbed the edges of the pan and brought it over to set it in the middle of the table. "Belly?" I called again, tipping my head to listen for her response. "Time to eat."

I heard a soft giggle, so I moved in that direction. I found Isabelle in the corner of the living room with Dog. She had her back to me and was holding something, which Dog was intently looking at as well. Whatever she had, it had captured both of their attentions.

"What did you find, love?" I asked as I stepped closer to peer over her shoulder.

She glanced at me as she pulled the item closer to her chest and drew up her knees like she was trying to hide it. "Nothing," she whispered, but her wide eyes gave her away.

"Isabelle," I said, using my best dad voice as I raised my eyebrows.

"Daddy, I..." Her voice trailed off and she jutted her little chin out. Then, slowly, she lowered her knees and let her hands fall into her lap. "Dog had this." She held up an ornament the size of a grapefruit. It was bright green with red sequins glued all over it.

My heart started to pound as I glanced over at Isabelle,

waiting for her reaction to it. Had she had a flashback? Did she remember that night?

But Isabelle didn't look uncomfortable. Instead, she looked reverent as she gently turned the ornament over in her hands. The look on her face was the exact look that Nicole used to get when she'd find the perfect Christmas decoration.

My chest squeezed at the thought of her mother. I'd done such a good job keeping her memory locked away in a box in my mind, and now, thanks to Clara, I was having a hard time keeping the lid closed. I cleared my throat and reached out my hand.

"It's not ours, Belly." I wiggled my fingers.

Isabelle looked up at me with her eyebrows knit together. "But, Daddy—"

"They're probably missing it. We need to find out who it belongs to." Even though I already knew who it belonged to. "Come on."

I watched her start to bring it closer to her chest before her expression softened and she slowly handed it over to me. Once it was securely in my grasp, I leaned down and scooped her up. She wrapped her arms tightly around me and buried her face into my neck.

Her little sob broke my heart, but I forced myself to stand strong. This really was the best thing for her.

When I got to the kitchen, I set the ornament on the top of the fridge—hopefully, out of sight, out of mind—and then bumped Isabelle a few times with the hopes of getting her to giggle. I could tell that she was fighting it, but on the third bump, she pulled back and squealed.

"Ready to eat?" I asked as I smiled down at her.

She returned the smile and nodded.

I dished up our plates and was moments from taking my seat next to Isabelle, when the sound of muffled music caused my entire body to freeze. The lyrics to "Rudolph the Red-Nosed Reindeer" carried to my ears, and my gaze snapped over to the nearby window.

Clara.

"Sit," I told Isabelle, who had shifted her weight like she wanted to climb off the chair. She gave a disgruntled *harumph* but thankfully stayed put.

I strode over to the window and looked out to see Clara standing in her front yard with a lit string of lights wrapped around her body. Her arms were stretched over her head like she was trying to detangle the mess. A speaker sat on the top of her deck railing, blasting her Christmas music.

"What is this woman doing?" I growled under my breath as I stared at her, hoping she'd look in my direction so I could convey just how angry she was making me.

As if the gods heard my wish, she flicked her gaze in my direction. She stared at me for a moment before she let the lights drop to the snow at her feet and cupped her hands around her mouth.

"Merry Christmas!" she shouted over the blare of her

music. Then she gave me the widest smile ever before turning her attention back to the lights.

I stared at her, anger rising up inside of me. Then I reached out, yanked the drapes closed, and turned my attention back to Isabelle, whose eyes were wide.

"She made her choice," I muttered as I joined my daughter at the table.

EIGHT
CLARA

I'm not going to lie, ticking off Mayor St. Grumpy-pants last night was like an early Christmas present to myself. The image of him at his window with his eyebrows raised and a stare that would rival the laser beam from the Death Star was now permanently etched in my brain. I counted it as a win as I watched him tug his curtains closed. But this morning I wasn't feeling so victorious.

I was currently standing in my open front door at the butt crack of dawn, wearing my nightgown and robe with my hair disheveled, and staring at some pencil pusher named Todd. He was wearing a black jacket over a grey suit and muttering to himself. He'd knocked at six a.m. and I'd done the stupid thing and answered.

I should have just pretended that no one was up.

I yawned as I watched him glance over his shoulder to my front yard and nodded his head like he was counting. I was proud of the work I accomplished yesterday. I'd spent the night decorating and got up half of what I'd brought to Grinchland. My decorations filled out the yard quite nicely, but I still had more to go. My goal was to have no empty spots when I was done.

And no one, not the mayor or his minion who used too much hair gel, was going to stop me.

"Did you not get the citation yesterday?" Todd asked as he turned his attention back to me.

A gust of wind blew past me, causing me to shiver, so I wrapped my robe tighter around my body. "I got it," I said matter-of-factly.

He flicked his gaze to mine. "So...you put up *more* things?"

"Decorations not *'materials.'* And yes, I did." I clenched my jaw. "This is still America. I have free will, don't I?"

Todd studied me for a moment. "Sure, but you do know that any sort of Christmas festivities have been banned here in Grinchland, right?"

I glanced over to Silas's house. "I've been informed," I said under my breath with my teeth clenched. "But I'm choosing to revolt against ridiculous laws that feel unconstitutional if you ask me." I folded my arms to punctuate my words.

When Todd didn't move to pat me on the back and give me an "attagirl", my confidence wavered just a bit. I didn't want to be the only person here fighting for Christmas. Though, based on the Grinchland residents I'd talked to, it was going to have to be a solo revolutionary.

"Don't you miss Christmas?" I asked, softening my gaze and attempting to plead with him on a human-to-human level.

A flash of something—sadness maybe—glinted in his eyes, but the next moment it was gone. He dropped his gaze to his jacket pocket and pulled out a pad and pen. "It's the way things are. There's no use fighting. Mayor St. Nick got the bylaws changed. I would suggest you just get on board. It'll help make everything go smoother." He started writing out what I could only assume was my second citation.

"What a jerk," I muttered under my breath. Only a jerk would change the laws to force people to not celebrate a holiday. Only a jerk would strongarm people into *not* doing something that felt as natural as breathing.

When Todd didn't respond, I glanced up. His expression was solemn. He wasn't defending Silas, but he also wasn't agreeing with me.

"You don't know?" he asked, his voice hushed and reverent.

That was not the response I'd expected from him. I frowned. "Know what?" My stomach sank just a bit. Did it have to do with his late wife? Isabelle's mom?

Todd studied the doorframe before he glanced up at me and shook his head. "It's not for me to say," he whispered.

Then why the heck did he say anything in the first place? I wanted to push him to cough up the story, but his jaw muscles were set, and I could tell from his countenance I wasn't going to get anything further from him. So I just waited while he finished filling out his notepad.

Finally, my curiosity got the better of me. "How did he go about banning Christmas in the first place?" I asked.

Todd paused and looked up at me. "He just got the town council to agree to change the bylaws. That's how most cities implement changes. You get enough people to vote one way and a decision is made."

"So...you're saying that if enough town council members agree to bring Christmas back, then it could become unbanned?" My wheels were turning now.

Todd's eyes widened. I could see a flash of regret on his face. "I'm not saying anything of the sort. I just answered your question as to how Mayor St. Nick got Christmas banned."

My smile was wide now, and there was nothing that was going to take it off. I wiggled my eyebrows at him. "I guess I'm just really good at reading between the lines." I gave him an exaggerated wink.

He knit his eyebrows together as he ripped the citation from the pad and handed it to me. "Just make sure that if you mention this to your neighbor that my name is not associated with it." His expression was serious as I took the citation from him. He held onto his end as if he wasn't going to release it until I agreed with him.

"These lips will be exactly what they sing about in Silent Night—silent," I said, pretending to lock my lips and throw the key over my shoulder.

He paused before he let go of the citation. "Okay," he said and then sighed. "I'm sure you're a nice person, but if you get the yard cleaned up and keep the noise to a minimum, then I won't have to come out here ever again."

I laughed. "I'm not doing that," I said as I shifted my weight so he could feel my attitude. I didn't come here to be told what to do.

"Clara—"

"Todd." I raised my eyebrows. "The mayor can't ban Christmas. He just can't." I paused. "When is the next town council meeting?" I couldn't just fight this from my front lawn. If I wanted sticking power, I was going to need to go to the source.

Todd sighed. I could tell that he didn't want to say but doubted that his silence would stop me. He was right.

"Tomorrow night," he said.

I grinned. "Perfect. I'll see you there."

"But—"

"No one will know that you're the one who told me." I tapped the edge of my nose and then gave him a wink.

He didn't look settled from my comment, but he didn't push me more. He was halfway down my stairs when he stopped and pointed to the two giant red ornaments I got last year.

"You have a twenty-two inch ornament set from

Balsam Hill?" Then he stopped and blinked like he hadn't expected to say those words out loud.

I parted my lips and jutted out my finger. "You're—"

"I didn't say anything," he said as he hurried down the rest of the stairs and across to his car. I was still waving my finger in his direction when he met my gaze as he backed out of the driveway.

That was an unexpected turn of events. He not only knew the brand of Christmas decoration I had on display, but he also knew that they'd sold out last year two days into December. They were *the* sought after decoration.

If Todd knew all of that, did that mean...he was a closeted Christmas fan?

I watched his car disappear around the corner before I stepped back and shut my front door. Maybe I wasn't the crazy one in this town; maybe it was Silas. I glanced at his house from my window, tapping my lips with my finger as my thoughts swirled.

Sure, my citations were starting to rack up. I now owed the town of Grinchland $240, which I did not have. But if I could get the town to agree that these rules were ridiculous and bring Christmas back, maybe they would waive the fees in gratitude.

"How many of you are living a lie?" I asked as I pictured the town and everyone I'd seen when I drove around yesterday. What had happened that made the entire town put their own holiday traditions aside and agree to banning an entire month?

Something big.

I sighed as I narrowed my eyes. No matter what, a mayor can't just impose his desires on a whole town. It was time a revolution began, and if I had to be the one to lead the charge, so be it.

My first act of full defiance was my outfit I picked out to wear to school. I decided not to go subtle. I went with my brightest, loudest—literally, it played Christmas music—dress I owned. With twinkling earrings and bright red lipstick, I looked like a very festive Ms. Frizzle.

"Perfect," I whispered as I turned side to side in the mirror. Silas St. Nick had no idea what was coming for him. This was war, and I was bringing out the big guns.

NINE
SILAS

Never in my life had a woman frustrated me as much as Clara Snow did. Nothing was getting through to her. I'd called Todd last night after I put Isabelle to bed, asking him to come as soon as he could this morning to give Clara a citation. I'd hoped it would convince her that I wasn't going to let this go, but instead of taking decorations down, she put up even more before she left for school.

When I saw her while dropping off Isabelle, my jaw hit the floor. Not only was she wearing blinking earrings shaped like Christmas lights, she had a dress that was so intense, it hurt to look at. Add the deep red lipstick and the strips of green and red tinsel that were clipped to her hair, and I was appalled.

Isabelle gasped, and at first, I thought my greatest fear had been realized. That she was finally remembering. But from the starstruck look in her eyes, I knew her reaction wasn't from fear but love. I was going to hear about Ms. Snow's outfit for days to come. My plan on keeping Christmas away from my daughter was no longer working—especially since this Christmas-obsessed person was now her teacher.

I sighed as I turned down our street. My days were already stressful as it was. With Clara added to the mix, I was ready for some dinner, a beer, and bed. But from the sight of multi-colored lights flashing on the road, I knew my night was just beginning. I slowed as I neared my house, fearing what I was about to see but knowing exactly what it was going to look like.

And I'd been right.

Clara had made quick work of decorating her lawn. There was not a square inch of open space to be seen. Santa stood next to his sleigh with reindeer leading the way. Large, tacky inflatable animals holding Christmas items waved in the wind with a giant nativity set in the center. Lights covered every possible surface of her house. She even had another Santa set on her roof.

This woman was a magician with how fast she got all this up.

Music blared from her house, and the lights danced along with the beat. I could only imagine what her electric bill was going to be this month. And with the sheer number of items that were simultaneously plugged in? I was surprised she hadn't blown the breaker.

I shook my head as I pulled into the driveway. Once

I'd parked my car in the garage, I gathered my things and got out. On days that I had late meetings, Mrs. Bloomburg from across the street came over to take care of Isabelle. She was a modest woman, and I wondered what she thought of the holiday monstrosity next door.

I shifted my briefcase to my other hand so I could open the back door. Once in the mudroom, I kicked off my shoes, hung my keys up, and then set my briefcase on the bench by the door.

"I'm home," I called out as I rolled my shoulders and then my neck. When no one answered, I made my way into the kitchen. The dishes were done and there was a faint smell of Italian seasoning lingering in the air. My mouth watered, wondering what Mrs. Bloomburg had made for dinner. She always fixed me a plate and left it in the fridge for when I got home.

"Daddy!" Isabelle's voice had me turning. She was running toward me from the dark living room. "Come see this." Her little hand found mine and she started tugging.

I let her drag me, and she didn't stop until we were standing in front of the living room window, the lights from Clara's house flashing against the couch, the floor, and all the walls. Mrs. Bloomburg sat on the armchair with her eyes wide.

"Evening," I said to Mrs. Bloomburg. "It's eventful out there."

She sputtered and nodded. "It's so…bright." She blinked as if to emphasize her statement.

"Yeah."

"It's magic," Isabelle whispered as she stepped forward and smooshed her face against the window. It was like she wanted to take in every inch of Clara's house.

"Peanut," I said as I grabbed a hold of her shoulder and pulled her back a few feet. Sure, this wasn't the TV, but that much light that close couldn't be good for the eyes.

"How do you feel about this?" Mrs. Bloomburg asked.

I glanced back at her. I widened my eyes and sighed. "I'm trying to deal with it. I told her about the laws, but she doesn't seem to care."

The music changed from Mariah Carey's "All I want for Christmas" with corresponding Christmas light show to Burl Ives singing "A Holly Jolly Christmas" which had a much slower melody, and I felt like I was less likely to have a seizure.

"Well, you're a stubborn man. I'm sure you'll manage." Her tone was light and full of affection as she slowly rose off the chair.

Out of anyone in Grinchland, she would know. When Nicole was alive, the two of them would sit on her porch drinking lemonade on the hot summer nights or hot cocoa as they watched the snow fall. I'm sure there were numerous times Nicole complained about me and my ways.

"I'll figure something out."

Mrs. Bloomburg nodded. "I have the confidence that you will."

I walked her to the front door. Once she had her jacket and scarf on, I held the door for her as she walked out onto the porch. Just as she stepped onto the doormat, she paused and bent down. When she straightened, she was holding a glittered lollipop.

"Did you drop this?" she asked, handing it over to me.

I took it from her and stared down at it. I shook my head. "No. But I have a feeling…" I glanced over at Clara's house. Was this part of her revenge? She was slowly going to drop decorations in my yard until I gave in and stopped citing her?

If that was her master plan, she was in for a rude awakening.

I glanced back over to Mrs. Bloomburg, who was studying me. She looked like she wanted to ask me a question but wasn't sure if she should. When she smiled and nodded toward her house, I realized she was never going to.

"All right, I'm going to head home." She held onto the railing as she started to descend the stairs.

"Can I walk you home?" I asked. I didn't want her to accidentally slip.

She paused and then nodded. "Might be for the best. My eyes aren't what they used to be, and those lights are messing with my depth perception."

I didn't wait for her to change her mind. I was down the stairs and to her side in a matter of seconds. She held onto my hand as we slowly walked down the pathway to the road. Once we were safely at her door, she patted my hand.

"I can take it from here," she said as she turned the handle.

"You sure?" I asked.

She nodded. "Yes, sir."

I told her goodbye and she returned the sentiment. When her door was firmly shut and locked, I shoved my hands into the front pockets of my slacks to conserve body heat as I hurried back across the street. Just as I got to my walkway, I stopped and stared over at Clara's house.

It made me angry that this woman thought she could just come in here and change everything because she didn't like the way things were done. We were a close-knit community. No one had complained when we outlawed Christmas. They knew they could celebrate it elsewhere. Why couldn't Clara just fall in line?

I shook my head as I pulled my phone out of my back pocket. If Todd and I couldn't talk some sense into her, maybe George could.

The phone rang three times when George's scratchy voice answered. "Sheriff speaking," he said.

I smiled as I turned away from Clara's house and hurried up the walkway to warmth. "George, it's Silas."

"What can I do for you, Mayor?"

"I need you to come write a ticket."

Thankfully, George didn't need a lot of convincing. I told him that as soon as he got here, he'd know what I was talking about. He didn't seem happy about it, but he said he'd stop by on his next round of patrolling.

I'd put Isabelle to bed, heated up and eaten my dinner, and I was enjoying my beer when George texted me that he was on his way. I was in bed in my pajama bottoms, so I grabbed my robe and headed downstairs. I sat in my lit up living room, waiting for the action to happen.

I was mid swig on my beer when George slowed in front of my house. I could tell his attention was on the scene playing out in Clara's lawn as soon as he pulled up.

My phone chimed with a text.

> Geez. Her electric bill must be in the hundreds.

> I'm sure it's astronomical

I downed the rest of my beer and set the empty can down on the side table next to me. I adjusted my weight on the couch as George pulled into the driveway and turned off his cruiser. I watched as he opened his door and climbed out. Once he rounded the hood, he paused. Then he went up her walkway until he got to her door.

A few seconds later, I saw her door open. They spoke and suddenly George was let inside. I frowned when the door shut and I could no longer see what was going on.

Twenty minutes later, George still hadn't come out and I was now pacing in my living room.

"How long does it take to write a ticket?" I grumbled under my breath.

Apparently for George, twenty-one minutes...now twenty-two.

I headed back up to my room, threw on a pair of jeans and tugged a sweatshirt over my head. It was unlikely, but I was going to check on George just in case Clara had decided to strangle him with tinsel and Christmas lights. It really was my duty as mayor.

I checked on Isabelle to make sure she was fast asleep. Then I grabbed my keys, locked the door, and headed over to Clara's. I couldn't tell if the house was quiet or not, the blasted music was too loud. How my daughter was sleeping through this should be studied.

When I got to her front door, I knocked—loud. I tapped my foot on her porch, my energy needing somewhere to go.

I had raised my fist to knock again when the door swung open. Clara was standing there with a smile on her face that suddenly dropped when she saw me.

"Mr. Mayor?" she asked as she glanced behind me and then met my gaze. "More citations to give me?"

I let out a forced laugh. "Is George here?"

She paused. "George? I don't know of a *George*..." Then she let out a laugh as she swung the door open to reveal the sheriff sitting at the dining room table. "Are you talking about *the life of the party?*" she said in an announcer voice.

"Mayor," George said as he moved to stand, cookie crumbs spewing from his mouth. He quickly wiped his upper lip with a sheepish expression. "I was just on my way out."

I quirked an eyebrow. Why did he look so suspicious? "I didn't mean to interrupt. I just wanted to check on you to make sure..."

Clara's eyes narrowed, and her stare felt like it was burning a hole into my soul. I shifted my weight as I scrambled to redeem myself. "I mean, I noticed your patrol car parked out front and wanted to make sure that everything was okay." I doubted she bought that correction at all. She knew that George was here because of me.

"So you're saying you had no idea that the sheriff was going to show up here?" She pointed her finger to the floor in emphasis.

I shrugged. "No clue."

"Huh." She paused. "So you had nothing to do with it?"

"Looks like it."

She stared at me a moment longer before she turned to George. "Can I make you a plate of cookies before you go?"

Her genuine smile was back, and for some asinine reason, a twinge of jealousy rushed through me when I realized that smile was for George alone. I blinked, startled by that reaction. I thought I must be drunk—even though

I'd only had one beer. If this was my reaction to alcohol, I was going to commit to being stone-cold sober.

"I don't know," George responded as he glanced down and hurried to wipe crumbs off his uniform.

I could tell from the sheer number of cookie remnants on his person that if I wasn't here, he'd need a wheelbarrow to transport all the cookies he'd accept.

"Don't change your mind on my account," I said as I folded my arms and leaned one shoulder against the doorframe.

Clara glanced over at me and then back to George. "You said Marigold would love the almond in the frosting." She leaned closer to George. "It's my magic ingredient." Her gaze met mine. "Multiple awards," she said, emphasizing the *p*.

"George isn't a reliable judge. I've seen him eat a questionable sandwich and call it a masterpiece."

Clara narrowed her eyes. "I promise you my cookies are much better than questionable sandwiches."

I shrugged. "I'll never know."

Clara huffed and pulled back, turning her attention back to George. "I'll pack you some cookies. I'm not taking no for an answer." She marched into the kitchen.

Now alone with George, I turned my attention to him. "What the heck?" I asked.

"I'm sorry, man. She invited me in, offered me cookies and hot cocoa." He shrugged. "What was I supposed to do?"

Was he serious? "Say no, write the ticket, leave." I tapped each finger as I spoke. "Easy."

He studied me. I could see that he wanted to agree with me, but his stomach was preventing him. I sighed, loud enough so he could hear.

"Did you at least write her a ticket?"

He paused. "I—"

"George." This was not how this evening was supposed to go.

He shrugged. "I'm sorry, man. Her cookies, they're evil." He scrunched up his face as he spoke the word, but the expression disappeared as soon as Clara entered with two full plates of cookies wrapped in cellophane.

"The second plate is for the station." She paused. "I want people in this town to get a little holiday cheer." She flicked her gaze over to me and then back to George. "And thanks for that list. It will be extremely helpful."

I frowned. "List? What list?"

Clara looked at me again before turning her attention back to George. "I'll see you tomorrow night. I'll be bringing more cookies with me too."

"Tomorrow night? What's tomorrow night, and why will she be seeing you?" I racked through my calendar and then my entire body went cold. "George," I said, my voice low. "What did you do?"

He winced as he hurried to grab the two plates of cookies from Clara. "Sorry, Silas. I gotta go." He turned, adjusted the plate in his left hand so he could turn the doorknob, and then sprinted out of the house like a bat out of hell.

When the door shut solidly behind him, I turned back to Clara. "What are you doing?" I glared at her. If she thought that she could just waltz into a town council meeting and get them to reverse the ban on Christmas, she had another thing coming.

"Just playing the game," she said as she shrugged before she folded her arms.

The likelihood of the entire council agreeing with her was slim to none, but she'd already got George on her side. There were only four people left. It wasn't out of the realm of possibility.

"You're leaving in a few months. Why are you doing this?" I pushed my hand through my hair. Things were good the way they were. Why was she so set on changing everything?

Her expression softened. She studied me before she sighed. "I guess there's another way. But only if you're up to it."

I didn't like that answer, but I wasn't going to do what I wanted to do—which was to tell her no. Thankfully, I'd worked in business long enough to understand that it was all in the negotiation. I'd let her lay out the terms and see if we could find common ground.

"What do you have in mind?"

TEN
CLARA

If you would have told me thirty minutes ago, when the sheriff was knocking on my door, that I would be standing here, about to negotiate with the Grinch, I would have said you were crazy.

There was no way in Rudolph's red nose I would have ever thought this would be a possibility. But here I was, with Silas in the palm of my hand.

He must have realized that I wasn't going to stop until I had all of the town council on my side. George had been easy to convince. He admitted that he missed Christmas and the treats that went along with it. It only took two cookies washed down with my award-winning hot chocolate, and he was ready to sign on the dotted line to reinstate Christmas.

He let me know that it would be harder to convince the other members but not impossible. With a list in hand of the town council and their favorite Christmas festivities, I was ready to take on Silas.

And I think he knew that.

But I was a simple person who preferred to take the route of least resistance. Instead of tromping all over Grinchland trying to find and convince the people in charge to see my side, I'd much rather go to the source. I was being given the opportunity to grow the heart of the person who'd banned Christmas in the first place, and I wasn't going to let that opportunity pass. It was the fastest and easiest route.

I'd seen the way Isabelle's eyes brightened when she saw me at school today, and I'd caught her trying to touch my earrings while she stood at my desk. I knew I needed to intervene. Grinchland and Isabelle needed Christmas. And I was certain that if I peeled back the layers of protection Silas had built up around his heart—he'd realize he needed Christmas as well.

But how did I convince the person who had outlawed Christmas in the first place that he actually needed it?

I glanced around, hoping to find my answer. When my gaze landed on the snow globes I'd bought with Abbie, I knew what I needed to do. I was going to have Silas experience all the traditions that I loved. There was no way he could do all these things and still uphold the ban in the end.

I could melt his icy heart. I was sure of it.

"I won't go behind your back and convince the council

to change the bylaws, if"—I held up my finger just as Silas's eyes narrowed—"you agree to participate in my Christmas traditions."

He scoffed. "No way."

I frowned. "Really?"

Resistance was to be expected. Convincing Silas was going to save me time, not be easier. So I shrugged. "I didn't peg you as a man who gives up."

"I don't give up."

"You're not going to negotiate?"

He sighed and shifted his weight. "Fine. What are you willing to offer me?"

"Spend the week with me."

He quirked an eyebrow.

"Doing Christmas things," I hurried to add. As soon as I spoke the no-no word, he pursed his lips like he was fighting the urge to tell me off. "At the end of the week, if you still hate Christmas and want it banned from your town, then I'll obey. I'll take down all of my decorations." I wrinkled my nose but continued. "I'll wear beige, and you will not hear another holly jolly word from me again."

He studied me. I could tell that he was mulling over my offer. I held his gaze, daring him to tell me no. This was the best option for both of us. I was so certain I would convince him to see my side that I almost changed the terms, but then decided to keep it to a week, just to be sure. Two days with me and he'd be dressing in gaudy Christmas sweaters and directing the Christmas choir.

"I have two conditions."

Whoa. I didn't think it would be that easy. "Okay," I said slowly.

"We don't involve Isabelle. And everything Christmas"—he spat the word like it tasted bad in his mouth—"stays at your house."

I didn't like the sound of that. "But—"

"Those are my terms." He shrugged. "Take it or leave it."

I frowned. I could fight him on this, *or* I could accept and spend the week trying to show him why his decision to ban Christmas was the wrong one. From the way his jaw was set and his blue eyes had greyed, I knew it would be better to push him later when he was full of my mulled cider and honey-baked ham.

"Fine," I said as I extended my hand. "You have yourself a deal."

I could feel his hesitation as he stared at my hand. I half expected him to back out. To claim this was all a joke and that he'd see me tomorrow at the town council meeting. Instead, he gripped my hand in his.

"Deal."

After we shook on it, he let go and dropped his hand back to his side. He glanced around as if looking for the next step when his gaze landed on the new paper snowflakes I'd made and hung in my front window.

He paused before taking a step closer. "Did you..." He frowned. "Did you turn your citations into snowflakes?"

I shrugged. "Maybe."

He glanced back at me. "You know you'll still have to pay those."

"Or I'm just that confident that you'll see my side of things once this is all over."

He furrowed his brow. "Um...but I just agreed. Right now."

I smiled. If he only knew. "I know."

"So you had no idea that I was going to go along with your crazy Christmas antics when you cut those up."

I quirked a shoulder. "Let's just say I had a hunch." Then I motioned toward him. "Looks like my hunch was right."

He studied me before he stepped away from the snowflakes. "So what is your plan?"

"You'll just have to find out." I grinned. "One week. Anything I want to do."

He paused, regret flashing in his gaze. "Within reason."

"That was not the agreement," I said pointing my finger in his direction. "I said *all* of my Christmas traditions."

He winced. "I'm assuming from all of this"—he waved his hands around the house—"you have a lot?" He ended that sentence with hope in his voice that I was going to calm his fears.

I chuckled. "You have no idea."

ELEVEN
SILAS

I woke up Friday morning with equal parts worry and regret. Worry for what the next seven days were going to bring me. Regret for even agreeing to Clara's plan in the first place. I had banned Christmas because it brought my family nothing but grief, and now I was stuck with the most Christmasy elf in Santa's workshop for the next seven days.

This was going to be hell.

"You have a plan," I muttered to myself for the hundredth time this morning. I was in the middle of making myself a cup of coffee to help me wake up.

The sound of Dog's doggie door had me looking over to see him prance inside. He looked content as he paused and glanced over at me. Ugh, to be a dog. Way less responsibilities. Way less…wait.

I stared at his neck. His collar was different. It was new and...Christmas themed.

"Dog, come," I said as I squatted down. He paused but then trotted over to me and sat. "What did that woman do to you?" I asked as I started to inspect the red-and-green checkered collar. Not only was it not my style, but as I shifted it, I could hear a jingle bell rattling against a metal name tag. I twisted the collar until I had the tag in hand.

I glanced down and my eyes bugged from my head.

"Blitzen?" I yelled and then pursed my lips. Had that woman seriously renamed my dog? "Your name is not *Blitzen*," I said as I started to feed the tongue of the collar through the clasp; it fell into my hand. I stuffed it into my pocket just as Isabelle appeared.

She was walking slowly, gracefully into the kitchen like she was feeling her outfit this morning and wanted me to notice.

"Wow," I whispered. "You look beautiful."

Isabelle took her time turning in a circle so I could see the full effect. She had her red dress on that I bought for the daddy-daughter Valentine's dance. She'd taped cut up pieces of green construction paper all over her dress. When she finished her rotation, she gracefully pulled her hair back to reveal that she had taped drawn Christmas lights to her ears for earrings.

She looked just like...Clara.

Part of me wanted to demand that she take it off. We didn't do Christmas in our house. But the other part of me, the one that supported his daughter no matter what, cheered and whistled to show my appreciation for her creativity. I never told Isabelle to change when it came to her style, and I wasn't going to start.

"I love it," I said as I walked over to her and planted a big kiss on her cheek. "What inspired you?"

Isabelle's smile was wide and infectious, and I found myself grinning back at her. "Do you think Ms. Snow will think it's pretty?"

I studied her. "I think she'll love it."

That seemed to be exactly what Isabelle needed to hear. "Good."

My fear of Christmas eliciting flashbacks for Isabelle seemed silly with her standing in front of me dressed like a miniature Ms. Snow. Suddenly, I felt ridiculous for listening to that child psychologist who'd said that to protect Isabelle I needed to remove everything that had to do with the night Nicole died. Was it possible that enough time had passed that I didn't need to worry anymore?

Maybe I'd taken things too far with this ban.

I shook my head. That was a ridiculous thought. I'd made a choice years ago to protect my daughter, and I was going to do just that. The human brain's a tricky thing. I would never forgive myself if something triggered her and she fell back into the dark abyss where I'd almost lost her. I couldn't protect her if the entire town was covered with decorations.

"Want some eggs and bacon?" I asked.

Isabelle had walked over to the mirror in the living room and was admiring herself. She was slowly turning side to side. "Okay," she said, not looking up.

After our scrambled eggs and crispy bacon were consumed, I rinsed the dishes and set them in the sink. I'd take care of them when I got home tonight.

Isabelle and I climbed into the car and I started the engine. Just as I was pulling out of the garage, I paused. Clara was currently walking to her car with her head down. She was wearing a less ostentatious dress today. It was blue with silver stars all over it. At the hem of the skirt was a shadowed depiction of the nativity scene.

She must have felt my gaze because, a second later, she raised her head and looked around. When her gaze caught mine, she smiled and waved. Her smile caught me off guard. For the first time since meeting her, her smile was genuine. She actually looked happy to see me.

Without thinking, I raised three fingers in acknowledgement.

And then I felt like an idiot. What was I doing? Why was I waving back? This was Clara—the woman who was trying to bring Christmas back to Grinchland.

I cleared my throat and focused my attention on pulling safely out of the driveway.

Whatever that reaction had been, it needed to never happen again. Lines had been drawn. This was war and Clara was the enemy. I needed to remember that.

I decided to stop and get doughnuts for me and

Isabelle on the way to school. That would give Clara enough time to park and get inside before we arrived, thus limiting the chance that I might run into her.

Thankfully, they gave us multiple napkins at the doughnut shop because I had to use all of them on Isabelle's face before we walked into school. She'd chosen a Boston cream long john and was wearing half the cream filling on her face. Once she was clean and ready, I held my hand out for her to grab so I could help her out of the truck.

She let me hold her hand as we walked into the building. Her step was lighter, and she kept glancing shyly at people like she was wondering if they were admiring her outfit. When we got to her classroom door, I stepped forward to grab the handle just as the door swung open, and Clara walked straight into me.

It startled both me and her, and before I could think, my hands were wrapping around her arms to keep her upright. Her eyes were wide as her gaze met mine, and for a brief moment, I stared at her. Being this close gave me a front-row seat to her copper-colored eyes with gold rings in them. They were framed with dark lashes, and she had a sprinkle of freckles across her nose. She smelled like vanilla and Christmas, and I found myself wanting to lean closer to inhale.

And then I realized what I was doing and dropped my hands like I'd just touched fire. "Sorry," I muttered as I took a step back.

Clara shook her head. "No, I should be apologizing. I was the one who ran into you. I should've looked through the window before I just barreled through." Her gaze drifted to Isabelle, who was standing with her chest puffed out in anticipation of Clara's praise.

That woman didn't disappoint. She ooh'd and aah'd over every detail Isabelle had put into her dress. Clara crouched down and made Isabelle twirl a few times so she could "get the full effect." Her adoration of my daughter did strange things to my chest.

I wasn't sure what to do about that.

When Clara straightened, her gaze met mine, and I took that moment to mouth, *thank you*. Her praise was exactly what Isabelle needed. Clara's smile turned shy as she nodded and mouthed back, *of course*.

There was a heaviness in the air that I didn't know how to interpret, and I wasn't sure I wanted to. Luckily Isabelle didn't seem to notice. She stepped towards the door that was now shut, glanced over her shoulder, and stated that it was time for me to go.

I started to ask her if she wanted me to walk her to her desk, but she just shot me a death stare before she yanked open the door and hurried into the classroom.

I was starting to see what my future would look like with her as a teenager, and it was terrifying.

Now alone in the hallway with Clara, I glanced over at her. She hadn't walked away yet, and I wasn't sure how to interpret that. She didn't look like she wanted to talk to me—she was looking everywhere but at me—so I wasn't sure if I was supposed to address her or not.

I hated that I felt awkward. I wanted to go back to how things were when we weren't talking. It was easier. I shifted my weight, and the heaviness of the collar shifting in my pocket drew my attention. Remembering that I'd removed it from Dog this morning, I pulled it out and held it up.

"Did you change my dog's name?" I asked.

Clara's face flushed as she studied the collar and then shifted her gaze back to me. Her expression turned sheepish, but she didn't move to take the collar from me. Instead, she just folded her arms and shifted her weight to one hip.

"It's not fair that his name is Dog," she said.

I studied her. Who was this woman? Why did she insist on coming into my life and blowing everything up?

When it became evident that she wasn't going to take the collar, I resorted to staring at her. "Is this part of our deal?" I asked. "Me changing my dog's name?" I quirked an eyebrow.

Clara fought a smile, and for the second time today, I found myself rejoicing that I'd elicited that reaction in her.

"Yes," she said with a resolute nod.

I studied her for a moment and then wrapped the collar up and stuck it back into my pocket. I'd promised to be a team player, and I was a man of my word, even if I thought what she had planned was ridiculous.

"Fine," I said as I emphasized the word.

"Good."

We stood there, staring at each other. Even though our conversation had ended, neither of us seemed eager to leave. Finally, the noise from her classroom rose, and she glanced over her shoulder and then back to me.

"I should get going," she said.

I nodded. "Same."

She turned and grabbed the door handle but then paused. "Come to my house tonight after the town council meeting. It's time for the festivities to begin."

I nodded. She smiled, pulled open the door, and disappeared. Now that I was alone in the hall, I blew out my breath and pushed my hand through my hair. Whatever that had been...had been unexpected.

I turned and started walking toward the front doors. For the first time this morning, the thought of spending time with Clara didn't fill me with dread.

For the first time, I was actually...excited.

TWELVE
CLARA

I managed to sufficiently distract myself after school. I made myself dinner. I ate said dinner. Then I took my time trying to decide what we were going to do for the night's festivities. My normal Friday night traditions in December were to watch a Christmas movie and string popcorn for garlands, so that was what we were going to do after we finished putting up the decorations in my house.

Decorating wasn't normally a task for December because, most times, everything was up by mid-November. And that was if I had put anything away to begin with. Much to Abbie's chagrin, most of my decorations stayed up all year round.

Decorating seemed like the perfect activity to ease Silas into my Christmas antics.

I set down the last box of Christmas decorations that

I'd brought in from the garage, blew out my breath, and glanced over to the grandfather clock in the living room. Why was I nervous? Time felt like it was both standing still and moving at lightning speed. In 20 minutes, Silas was supposed to be knocking on my front door.

I was in the midst of popping my sixth bag of popcorn when I heard a knock at the door. I glanced at the clock to see that time really did fly when you were distracted. It was 8:45, which meant it had to be Silas. But in this town, I never really knew.

Butterflies erupted in my stomach as I hurried to wipe the popcorn butter off my hands before I made my way to the front door. I told myself those butterflies were just nerves. I was inviting the Grinch into my house, and I was about to share what I loved most about the holiday with him. But my head knew better. I literally heard the words, *girl, please* echo in my head.

I pushed both thoughts out of my mind. This was neither the time nor place to try to dissect what had happened this morning between me and Silas, so I wasn't going to try. I was going to focus on the task at hand, and only that.

I turned the handle and pulled the door open, getting ready to greet him with a flourish, but when he quickly pressed his finger to his lips, I obeyed. He pointed to Isabelle, who was wrapped in a blanket and passed out on his shoulder.

I pressed my fingers to my lips and nodded. Then I

motioned for him to follow me. I held the door open as he passed through to the foyer, kicking his shoes off as he entered. With the door now shut, I led him through the house and into my bedroom. The lights on the Christmas tree in there were on, creating a warm ambiance. I pulled back my covers and patted the bed.

Silas was gentle as he lowered her to the mattress. She whined and wiggled for a moment before she stilled. It was doing strange things to my insides, watching him sweep back the hair that had come loose from her braid, before he studied her to make sure she was comfortable and then straightened.

When his gaze met mine, I realized that I had been staring, so instantly I looked away.

What are you doing? the voice from earlier hissed in my ear.

Being an idiot, apparently.

"She good?" I whispered after I'd gathered my wits and turned my attention back to Silas.

He was still studying Isabelle. It felt like an eternity before he glanced up and nodded. "I think we're good." He glanced around my room, and I watched as the realization that he was in *my* room passed over his face.

His cheeks reddened and he looked panicked when he met my gaze.

"Let's leave her," I said as I began to shepherd him to the door. I wasn't messy, but I also wasn't a clean freak. The last thing I needed was for him to see my bra dumped on the floor because I'd been too tired last night to put it away.

Once we were out in the hallway, I quietly closed my door until it was open just a crack. That way, he'd hear Isabelle if she got up, but she wouldn't be bothered by us moving around.

I glanced up to see Silas studying me. The narrowness of the hallway forced him close to me, and suddenly, I wasn't just looking at him, I was looking *up* at him. I could feel his body heat and smell his scent. It was a mixture of rough, outdoorsman with the scent of clean laundry.

This interaction was too intimate.

In an effort to focus on something else, I dropped my gaze to his chest and gave his outfit a once-over. He was wearing a black sweatshirt and a pair of grey sweatpants. He went more casual this evening, a stark difference from the suits I'd thought he lived in.

"What?" Silas was frowning when I glanced up. Finally, an expression I recognized.

I shook my head. "Nothing." I turned and made my way through the hall and back into the kitchen to find that the microwave had finished. I was pulling out the bag of popcorn when Silas appeared in the doorway.

"What were you staring at?" he asked as he glanced down at his clothes.

"Nothing," I said again. I pulled open the sides of the bag and then dumped the popcorn into the bowl on the counter.

"It's not nothing. You were staring at my clothes with a strange look." He folded his arms and rested his shoulder on the doorjamb. He really wasn't going to let this go.

I sighed. "Do you own anything that's not basic?"

He frowned. "Basic?"

I crumpled up the now empty popcorn bag and tossed it into the nearby garbage. I assessed the popcorn pile and concluded that we had enough.

"You know, brown, white, black." I ticked the colors off on my fingers and emphasized the last color by pointing to his sweatshirt.

"What's wrong with *basic*?" he asked as he once more glanced down at his clothes.

I shook my head. "Nothing."

He narrowed his eyes.

"Besides, I can solve"—I waved my hand in his direction—"all of this." I smiled at my ability to mirror the gesture that he made toward me on the first day back at him.

He paused as his expression grew contemplative. "I never agreed to having you dress me."

"You agreed to everything," I said as I waggled my finger at him.

He shook his head. "I do believe my words were, *within reason*."

I blinked, startled that I was going to have to explain this to him. "A Christmas sweater *is* within reason."

His eyes practically bugged from his head. "Nope. No

way. I am *not* wearing one of those tacky sweaters." He brushed down his sweatshirt. "I have an image to uphold. Besides, I like my clothes."

I gave him another once-over and shrugged. "Eh. They're boring."

"I'm okay with boring."

I grinned at him. "For now. Give me a few days and you'll be singing a different tune."

He eyed me and then glanced around the kitchen. "Does your holiday tradition include eating an obscene amount of popcorn?" He nodded toward the overflowing bowl in front of him.

"This is for the second portion of the night."

"There are...portions?"

I nodded. "Yep." And then, without thinking, I reached forward and grabbed his hand so I could guide him to the living room, where the night was going to start.

At first, touching him felt natural. But when I started moving and he didn't, I paused and glanced back to see him standing there, stiff as a board, staring at our hands. That's when I realized what I'd done. I instantly dropped his hand and took a step back.

"Sorry," I muttered. There were two emotions going through me right now. I was trying not to be embarrassed that I might have overstepped. That reaction paired perfectly with feeling offended that he was so disturbed by my touch. There had to be huggers in his life. A large section of the population liked physical contact.

Silas stretched and clenched the hand I had grabbed before he glanced up. "It's fine," he said.

That was an obvious lie. He looked like he was trying to exorcise my touch right off his skin. It made me feel *so* good.

"Won't happen again," I said and then decided the best move was to just pretend it hadn't. I kept a good three feet away and waved for him to follow. "Come with me."

I led him into the living room. He stayed near the doorway while I walked further in. As soon as I got to the bins of decorations, I took the lid off the first one. When he didn't approach, I glanced over at him.

"Come on," I said before I chuckled. "I'm not going to bite."

He looked like he didn't believe me, but after a few seconds he approached. "What are we doing?" he asked cautiously.

I pulled out the Mr. and Mrs. Santa Claus gnomes and held them up. "We're decorating."

His expression was deadpan as he stared at me, and then at the bin. "Was this your plan all along? To have me be your little elf?" He folded his arms across his chest.

I just smiled. "My little *elf*?" I asked, loving that he was using a Christmas analogy with me. I felt triumphant. It meant I had already begun cracking his icy exterior.

His cheeks reddened as he held up a finger. "What, no," he said quickly. "I didn't mean to say that."

I held up the gnome couple and started to slowly turn

around the room as I looked for the perfect place to set them. "And yet"—I sighed and tipped my head—"you did." And then inspiration struck.

The second shelf in the bookcase next to the TV was the perfect place for these two. I gave him a knowing look as I passed by him.

I could see that he was fighting with himself, so I continued decorating while he came to terms with the effect I was having on him. Finally, he seemed to have given up trying to deny what he said and slowly stepped up to the bin. He shuffled some of the items around like he didn't know what to do.

"Hey, hey," I said as I took the porcelain teddy bear wearing a Christmas scarf with presents at his feet from his hands. I'd had enough of Silas manhandling him. "Be nice to Cinnamon."

He watched with equal parts curiosity and horror as I gently set Cinnamon down in the palm of my left hand before bringing him up to eye level.

"Cinnamon?" he asked.

I nodded and glanced over at him. "What? You don't name your Christmas decorations?" I brushed off the top of Cinnamon's head and then blew on him a few times.

Silas looked at me like I had two heads. "No."

"Right, because you don't have Christmas decorations," I said. I walked toward the shelf that the gnome couple was on and set down Cinnamon. "That's kind of a prerequisite."

Silas folded his arms. "Even if I did have one, I wouldn't name it." He shook his head.

"I highly doubt that." I snorted as I made my way back to the bin. "If you had a Christmas decoration, you would name it, it's the law." I narrowed my eyes. "And you have great respect for the law." I made sure my voice was light even though the words I spoke were heavy.

He just stared at me.

"How about we make a wager?" I turned to face him with my hand extended.

He flicked his gaze down to my hand and then back up. "What did you have in mind?"

I tapped my chin, mentally running through my decorations. I'd managed to make most of them fit, I just couldn't put up Pudgie the penguin. I'd run out of outlets.

"If you put up my inflatable penguin in your yard and you don't feel the urge to name him by the end of the seven days, I'll..." I glanced around the room, looking for something I could offer him. But he'd made it clear he absolutely didn't want anything I owned.

"You'll get Isabelle an invite to Catalina's party."

I glanced over at him. "What?"

He was staring at the ground with his hands shoved into the front pockets of his sweatpants. His jaw was set and I could tell that this bothered him.

"Catalina Turnbow. She's having a party that all the kids in the class have been invited to, except Isabelle." He paused. "I can have an abrasive personality, and her mom...isn't too fond of me. I'm worried that's why she's excluded my daughter. If her fun, loving teacher is the one who raises a concern, maybe you can get Janice to invite Belly."

Out of everything he could ask for, this was what he wanted? He had to know that I would never tolerate this kind of behavior from parents. Not inviting all the kids from a classroom was not okay.

"Yes, of course," I said as I shook my head. "But you didn't need to make it part of this deal. I would have done it regardless."

He studied me for a moment and then shrugged. "I don't like owing anyone anything."

I paused. "Because you're the mayor?"

"Something like that."

Well, if that was what he wanted, then I could play this game. "All right. You put up the inflatable penguin in your yard for seven days. If at the end you haven't named him, then I will talk to Catalina's mom about why Isabelle was excluded from the party and remind her what common decency dictates."

Silas paused, like he was mulling over what I'd offered, before he stepped forward and took my hand like this was a business deal he wanted to close. Tingles erupted across my skin, so I dropped my gaze, hoping he didn't notice that his touch had brought a reaction out in me. After all, it wasn't like it meant anything. I was just excited that my plan to change the Christmas-hating mayor into a contributing member of Whoville was working.

Needing to break the ice, I leaned toward him before he let go of my hand and whispered, "I'll talk to her mom as soon as I see her."

He stilled before he glanced down at me, bringing his face inches from mine. He held my gaze for a moment, and there was something there. An ache. A pain. A rawness that I related to. But it was gone with a blink.

"Thank you," he said, his voice deep and gruff. He dropped my hand and took a step back. His gaze snapped to the bin. "Decorations?"

I nodded. "Decorations."

THIRTEEN
SILAS

Something had shifted between me and Clara. Something that I never in my wildest dreams could have imagined. Something deep and abiding. And when I thought about it, it took my breath away. It startled me in a way I hadn't anticipated.

It was the realization that Clara was even more Christmas crazed than she'd originally let on.

We were an hour in and still unloading her decorations onto every surface of Linda's house. Despite the fact that the shelves were already bursting at the seams, more bins kept appearing with more decorations that needed homes. I felt like she was a magician pulling doves from a hat.

Clara hadn't noticed me staring at her as she unclipped the lid to another bin and pulled it off. She was recounting the story behind the glass Christmas star that I'd just unpacked. Every item in her possession had a story to it. A memory so sacred that I could hear the reverence in her voice.

It was endearing that she cared so much. Especially since I spent most of my life trying *not* to care too much about anything. After I lost Nicole, I realized that everything could be taken away from me, so I tried not to get attached.

Houses could be sold. Things could be replaced. The only thing that mattered to me was Isabelle. She was the one caveat to my *I don't give a shit* attitude. She was the one thing that kept my feet on the ground. Without her, I'd have moved to the mountains and lived the rest of my life in seclusion.

I was lost in my own thoughts when I realized that Clara was staring at me. I glanced over at her and then around the room, wondering what I had missed. When had she stopped talking? My ability to keep my mind grounded and my focus sharp had started to slip ever since this woman moved in next door.

I was losing my edge.

"What?" I asked as I rolled my shoulders, hoping to appear cool and aloof.

She shook her head. "Nothing." She started unpacking a porcelain nativity set. "I get it."

I frowned. "Get what?" When she didn't answer, I took a step closer to her. "Get what?" I dipped down, trying to meet her gaze. Sure, I thought that her attachment to these items was a bit much, but I understood it.

She glanced up at me and shrugged. "You just have the same look on your face that everyone gets when I talk about the history behind all"—she waved her hand around the room—"of this stuff." She turned her attention back to the bubble-wrapped item she was holding, grabbed the edge of the wrapping, and pulled it up. Baby Jesus in a manager came tumbling out onto her hand. She glanced up at me. "You're judging me," she whispered.

I knit my eyebrows together. "I'm not judging you." Sure, the sheer amount of holiday items she had was ridiculous, but that didn't mean I judged her for it.

Some people gambled to deal with loss. Some people drank. Even though Christmas decorations were the last thing on earth I would ever surround myself with, I understood why she did it. She was coping. I wasn't sure with what, but I had a suspicion.

She sighed as she set baby Jesus next to the shepherd and the wise man she'd already unwrapped. "That's okay. I'm used to it. Most people think I'm out of my mind, I'm too much, I'm crazy." She stuck out her tongue and wiggled her head to emphasize her statement,

"Most people are idiots." I shrugged. "I stopped living to please people a long time ago." I shook my head. "Besides, you're not crazy or out of your mind. You're sentimental. There's a difference." I reached into the bin and grabbed one of the bubble-wrapped nativity figurines to help her.

Clara may have quirks that I didn't understand and didn't necessarily like, but that didn't make her wrong. In my experience, it was the people passing moral judgment who were wrong.

I'd unrolled Joseph and was working on Mary when I realized that Clara hadn't spoken. When I glanced up, she was staring at me with her eyebrows drawn together.

"What?" I asked as Mary fell into my hand. I laid the bubble wrap on top of the sheet I'd just taken off of Joseph. "Why are you staring at me like that?" I set Mary next to Joseph and got another figure out.

Clara blinked a few times before she shook her head. "It's just...no one's ever said that to me before. I've always just been the overly zealous Christmas friend." She tucked her hair behind her ear, her cheeks flushing as she met my gaze.

I wasn't sure what to say to her confession. I was already learning too much about the woman who was trying to bring back Christmas. She'd made it clear since the moment she stepped into Grinchland that she had no respect for the town or its rules. So while I could sympathize with her and the plight of having everyone misunderstand her intentions, it didn't mean I wanted to get close to her.

It didn't mean that I wanted to be friends.

I had a job to do. To keep the structure of Grinchland

safe, I needed to keep our relationship revolving around one thing: fulfilling this agreement so that in seven days normal life could resume in Grinchland. A life that was Christmas-less.

Neither of us spoke again as we finished unwrapping the nativity set and perched it precariously on the edge of Linda's piano. There were a few more items to take out, and I attempted to find spots for them while Clara stacked the bins inside of each other and hauled them off to the spare bedroom.

When she returned, I expected her to say that day one was over and I could go back to my house. Instead, she told me to follow her into the kitchen, where she instructed me to bring the huge bowl of popcorn into the living room while she went to find needles and thread.

I wanted to tell her that I'd had just about enough holly jolly for one day, but then I remembered the goal. Seven days and then this woman would let Christmas go. I just had to stick it out for one week, and then my life could return to normal.

Twenty minutes into stringing popcorn, I almost called it quits right then and there. My fingers felt like pin cushions, that's how many times I pricked them. The movie *Elf* was playing in the background, and while Clara loved it—she kept swatting my arm right before she would break out into laughter—I was...tolerating it.

And I was playing fast and loose with the word *tolerate*.

I was halfway done filling my string with popcorn when I glanced up to see Clara's eyes were glued to the screen and she was picking up pieces of popcorn and *putting them in her mouth.* My gaze drifted down to her popcorn garland to see she'd only completed a fourth of what I'd accomplished.

I waited until she was bringing more popcorn to her lips before I grabbed a piece and chucked it at her. "We're stringing, not eating."

Her hand was suspended in front of her mouth when she brought her gaze over to me. Then slowly, ever so slowly, she slipped the popcorn into her mouth.

I sighed. This was going to take forever if she kept eating the supplies.

I pricked my thumb, again, so I draped the string over my lap and leaned back while I pressed hard on my skin to stop the bleeding. "Why are we doing this?" I nodded toward the tree in the corner of the room. "You already have a decorated tree."

Clara looked at me like I was an alien with two heads. "I have *one* tree."

She said the word *one* like I should know exactly why my question was a stupid one.

"Isn't it normal to have just *one* tree?"

Clara laughed. It was loud and genuine, and my stomach flip-flopped at the sound. First, there had been her smile earlier today at the school. Now her laugh. I didn't like how I was reacting to her. I didn't want to see her as anything other than the annoying woman next door who was trying to bring Christmas back to a town that had already cancelled it.

"Not for me," she said as her laughter died down to a giggle.

That I could believe. Nothing seemed to be enough for this woman.

"Why do you like Christmas so much? And why is it always *this* holiday? I've never seen someone go this insane over the Fourth of July."

Clara poked her needle into the armrest of the couch and shifted so she could sit facing me. I wanted to take my question back. I hadn't meant to distract her. I wanted off of this crazy Christmas merry-go-round, and I feared that would never happen when I kept stupidly engaging her in conversation.

She crisscrossed her legs in front of her and rested her elbows on her knees. She steepled her fingers before pressing them to her lips while looking deep in thought.

"Thing is, it's not so much Christmas that I love. It's... everything. The decorations, the songs, the people."

I frowned at her last word. I actively avoided people when I could. If Clara noticed, she didn't say anything. Instead, she continued to stare off with a dreamy expression.

"It's just that this time of year, everything is better." She glanced over at me and pulled back. My expression must have accurately depicted my emotions because she gave me a once-over before she knit her eyebrows together. "Obviously, you don't feel the same. What about you? Have you always hated Christmas so much you wanted to ban it?" Her tone had turned cheeky as she reached out and smoothed the material of her couch with her hand.

There was so much to unpack in that question, and I doubted she wanted to hear any of my reasons. There was also the little fact that I didn't talk about Nicole anymore, and I wasn't about to start with her, so I just shrugged. "I used to tolerate it."

I could feel Clara's gaze on me.

"You obviously don't tolerate it anymore," she said, her voice soft as she shifted her focus back to the couch cushion. She was quiet for a second before glancing up at me. "So you're telling me that you've never had a memorable Christmas? One that you'd never forget?"

Christmas lights. Decorations. Snow...sirens.

I did have a Christmas that I would never forget no matter how much I wanted to.

The holiday just happened to correspond with the night my life had changed forever. It was the reason my wife died, and I lived in constant fear that my daughter would return to her despondent state. I'd lost one important woman in my life, I wasn't going to let Christmas take another. If I could save my daughter by getting rid of a holiday, I'd make that choice every time.

I stared at my hands. Then I looked at the popcorn that I'd been stringing before I slowly swept my gaze around the room, tuning into the music and movie playing next to me.

That's when realization dawned. What was I doing?

"I, um..." I pulled the garland off my lap and stood, brushing the popcorn bits from my pants. "I need to go," I said. I didn't wait for Clara to respond. Instead, I turned and headed back to her room to get Isabelle.

"Um, okay," Clara said as I heard her scramble to follow me.

I didn't stop as I made my way through her house. As soon as I reached Isabelle, I hoisted her up and helped her adjust so her head was resting on my shoulder.

I could hear Clara behind me, but I didn't address her. She was following me as I left her room in pursuit of the front door. Just as my hand found the handle, her voice stopped me.

"Did I do something wrong?"

The quiet way she spoke caused me to pause. I stared hard at the oak door in front of me before I glanced over my shoulder to see that Clara's eyes were wide as she stared up at me.

A lot of thoughts rolled around in my mind, but I fought every one of them. Clara wasn't here to stay. She had an expiration date. Plus, this was Grinchland—and if my plan worked, it would stay that way. We were two sides of a coin. Complete opposites.

She didn't belong in my world like I didn't belong in hers.

"I've just had enough Christmas spirit for one night." I turned the handle and pulled open the door. Just as I stepped out onto her porch, I stopped. I didn't want to leave her like this. There was a part of me that wanted to say more, I just wasn't sure what I should say.

Without thinking, I turned to face her. "It was an adequate night." I held her gaze for a moment before I turned and hurried down her steps.

Thankfully, she didn't call after me. I felt her stare as she lingered on her porch. I kept my gaze forward, and as I made my way up my walkway, the sound of her door shutting sounded in the distance.

Once I was inside my house, I blew out my breath.

There was so much for me to unpack from my time with her, but that was the last thing I wanted to do. Right now, I was going to put Isabelle to bed, change into my pajamas, and crawl into bed. Then I was going to sleep.

I would save thinking about Clara for tomorrow.

FOURTEEN
CLARA

A good night's sleep did nothing for the confusion I felt after Silas clammed up and skedaddled from my house. I thought he was having fun. After all, *I* had been having fun. How could I not? I was watching the classic Christmas movie, *Elf*, I was stringing popcorn for my next tree, and all my decorations were finally out of their bins.

For Clara Snow, that was a quintessential December night.

Silas might not have been enjoying himself, but he had definitely been tolerating it. There were even a couple of times here and there when it felt like Silas was complimenting me. Understanding me. Speaking to me in a way that no one had spoken to me before.

Then it all came crashing down. Suddenly, he was scooping up Isabelle, rushing through my house, and disappearing out the door like Santa running late to drop off presents.

There was no explanation for his hasty exit, and I was left wondering what the heck had just happened.

So I went to bed. Gran always said that things made more sense in the stark light of morning. But as I lay on my bed, staring up at the ceiling that was softly illuminated by the Christmas tree in the corner, I was still at a loss.

Silas's sudden shift didn't make sense.

Maybe he was the kind of guy that had a hard limit. Once he got to a certain amount of Christmas joy, he was done. He'd been moments away from overheating and needed to return to his dark and cheerless house to cool down.

I nodded. "That's it," I said, trying to convince myself, even though I knew, deep down, I was wrong.

I didn't want to acknowledge it, but I knew what the true explanation was. He'd seen a little too much of my crazy and had had enough. It happened every time I tried to let someone in. They either tried to change me or left without a word.

Silas was no different.

I groaned as I grabbed a nearby pillow and covered my face with it. Even the men who were forced to spend time with me couldn't stick around. I shook my head against the soft fabric. I was going to die alone.

My plan for the day was the only thing that forced me

out of my funk, off my bed, and into the shower. Once I was clean and fully awake, I shut off the water and grabbed a towel. After I dried off, I wrapped the towel around my body and stepped out onto the plushy bathmat with *Merry Christmas* written in cursive.

I settled on a plain green sweater and a pair of dark jeans. My plans included Isabelle, and I didn't want my obnoxious Christmas clothes to be the reason Silas rejected my ideas. He said Isabelle couldn't participate in *Christmas*-related activities. The things I had planned didn't have to be categorized as *Christmas*.

I was excited to spend the day with that little girl. I almost cried yesterday when I saw her outfit. The fact that she'd mimicked me was the best compliment anyone had ever paid me. Ever.

And the fact that Silas let his daughter pick such an outfit even though he was vehemently opposed to Christmas...well it endeared him to me a tad bit more.

It was hard to want to take him down when he could be so sweet with his daughter. Why couldn't he just be a grinch to everyone? It would make hating him that much easier.

After blow-drying my hair and applying some makeup, I turned off my lights and headed out into the kitchen, where I grabbed a granola bar and a Christmas cookie. I was chewing while I slipped on my boots, and I finished off my cookie before I pulled on my jacket and tied my least Christmas-looking, yellow scarf around my neck.

I shouldered my purse and headed out the door. When I passed by my garage, I slipped inside to grab Pudgie.

The sun's rays were peeking through the branches as I made my way up Silas's walkway. It was such a shame that he hated Christmas. His house was just begging for some decorations. He really had the perfect place for it. It was every Christmas fanatic's dream.

"Such a waste," I whispered as I climbed the front steps.

I had to knock a few times before the door opened. Isabelle stood there in a Princess Tiana nightgown, and there was a dusting of what looked like flour across her nose. Her hair was pulled back into a braid, but a night of tossing and turning had matted up chunks of it.

"Ms. Snow!" Isabelle exclaimed as she stepped to the side to let me in.

"Hey, sweetie," I said as I glanced around, not sure if I should wait until Silas invited me in. "Your dad home?"

She glanced behind her toward what I could only assume was the kitchen. "Yeah," she said as she started to walk away from me.

Not knowing what to do, I stepped into the foyer and turned to shut the door behind me. "Can you let him know that I'm here?" There was no way I was going further inside without being invited.

"Belly, that was not okay." The door to the right past the staircase opened, and a flustered, *shirtless* Silas came walking out. His hair was disheveled, his jaw was unshaven, and his chest...

Crap.

His broad shoulders, muscular chest, and abs... I didn't need to know that he has abs under all of his pretentious suits. Why couldn't he be anything but perfect? He looked like he was chiseled by the gods.

"Ms. Snow?"

I snapped my gaze up. His eyes were wide and his eyebrows were raised as he stared at me in disbelief.

"Isabelle let me in," I said as if that was going to justify why I was so obviously ogling him.

He glanced over his shoulder and then turned back to me. "Oh." He studied me for a moment. "Belly! What did I tell you about answering the door?" And then, as if he suddenly realized that he was standing there shirtless, his smile turned sheepish. "Sorry. Belly spilled pancake mix all over my shirt." He moved his hands like he was trying to decide if he should cover up or not.

I nodded. "Oh." I wasn't sure if I should drop my gaze or keep it focused on Silas. If I looked away, would he think that I was embarrassed? Or if I kept looking at him, would he think that I liked what I was seeing?

This was all too complicated for me, and my brain was short-circuiting, so I just stood there like an idiot. Then I remembered that I was holding Pudgie. "Brought this over," I said as I leaned forward and set the penguin down next to the front door.

I could feel Silas's gaze on me, and when I straightened and looked back at him, he startled as if he'd been snapped out of a trance.

"I'll go get dressed," he said as he walked forward to the entrance of the staircase and then took the stairs two at a time.

I wasn't sure what to do, so I just stood there, facing the staircase. My mind instantly went to how I would decorate it. Magical was the only way to describe it.

"Um, can you help Belly clean up in the kitchen?" Silas suddenly appeared at the top of the stairs. His gaze met mine, and all I could do was nod.

Yes. Good. A job. That was what I needed.

"Absolutely," I said as I kicked off my boots and started to unzip my jacket.

Isabelle and I had cleaned up the spilled pancake mix with paper towels and were in the middle of mopping when Silas joined us. His hair was damp, his face was freshly shaven, and he was wearing a black sweater and dark jeans. I shook my head. I was determined to see him in color before our seven days were over.

He glanced around and noticed that I was watching him. He met my gaze for a moment before he turned his attention to Isabelle. "Looks great, peanut," he said as he crossed the space between them and planted a kiss on the top of her head.

She paused and then wrinkled her nose. "You smell weird."

Silas's cheeks reddened as he glanced over at me. "It's just my cologne. You've smelled it before." He reached out to tousle her hair, but she dipped and dodged his hand.

Isabelle shook her head. "I never smelt that before in my life," she said as she swished her hand in front of her nose.

Silas glanced around like he was looking for an out. I couldn't help but smile. He was embarrassed. Five-year-olds will do that to you. They have a way of making the proudest in society crumble with self-doubt.

"You missed a spot," he said as he pointed his finger to a spotless section of the kitchen floor.

Isabelle dragged the mop across the floor in a squiggly pattern, cleaning the spot that he'd claimed she'd missed.

"Ms. Snow helped me," Isabelle said as she glanced back to me and smiled.

Silas looked relieved that we were now officially off the topic of his cologne. "I know," he said as he glanced over at me once more. Then he mouthed, *thank you*.

I just smiled and shrugged. "Happy to help." Then I paused. "Actually, I was hoping it would put me in your good graces."

Silas eyed me. "What did you have in mind?"

I took a step to the side and motioned with my head

for him to follow. Isabelle didn't seem to notice as she continued drawing with the mop.

"As you know, it's day two."

His eyebrows went up, stopping any more of my proposition from flowing. "I didn't think we'd be doing this on the weekends. You know, with Isabelle being around and all."

"I was hoping we could take her out with us today." I nodded discreetly toward Isabelle.

Silas flicked his gaze toward his daughter. "I don't know," he said slowly.

I waved toward my clothes. "Look, I'm just wearing plain green. And the things I have planned aren't reserved just for Christmastime." I held up three fingers. "Scouts honor, I promise the word that shall never be said *will* not be said while we are out." Then I leaned in and started to spell it out. "C-h-r—"

"I know what the word is," he said. He was watching Isabelle, and I could see the internal battle raging. He finally sighed. "All right, she can come with us," he said as he glanced back at me.

I didn't fight my excitement this time. I leaned in, grabbed his forearm, and shook it while I squealed. I'd completely forgotten that he didn't like to be touched, and his entire body froze. It wasn't until I let him go that he finally started moving.

"Sorry," I said, making a mental note to *not* touch Silas again.

He shook his head before pushing his hand through his hair. "It's okay," he said, his voice low. He took in a deep breath. "So what are these Christmas-but-not-Christmas activities we're going to be doing?"

I tapped my lips with my forefinger. "You'll just have to wait and see."

FIFTEEN
SILAS

I really needed to stop agreeing to Clara's plans if she uses the phrase, *you'll just have to wait and see*. Every time I let her lead, I found myself doing things I definitely did not want to do.

I knew this was a bad idea, and yet, I'd not only agreed to let Isabelle come, but I'd also agreed to let Clara drive after she'd insisted. I really hoped she'd keep her promise by keeping Christmas out of our plans. Isabelle seemed to be reacting well to the holiday cheer Clara had already let into our small town, but I wasn't going to trust a full baptism into the holiday season.

And I didn't believe that Clara was capable of anything short of a full baptism.

"So, where are we going?" I asked for what felt like the hundredth time today.

I was sitting in the front seat next to Clara while

Isabelle sat in the seat behind me. I glanced around at my surroundings. "And why are we headed to Jordan?" It was two towns over.

Clara shook her head. "I told you it was surprise. Why do you keep trying to ruin it?" She shot me an annoyed smile before she flipped on her blinker and took a left.

I glared at her. "This isn't fair, you know. Everything has to be a surprise with you."

She laughed. "Are you shocked? My favorite holiday is the one day a year you give the most surprises." She shrugged. "I love seeing people's reactions."

"It's not fair."

She shrugged. "I think you'll get over it."

She began to slow, so I glanced over my shoulder to see a sign that said *McCall's Christmas Trees next left*. My eyes bugged as I glanced over at her.

"You promised." I hated that I felt so betrayed by her. "This goes against our agreement."

"It doesn't," she started, and I whipped my gaze back to her. "Hear me out." She glanced around the car and finally pulled out a receipt from the cupholder and handed it to me. "What would you call this?"

I gingerly picked it up, confused as to where she was going with this. "An old receipt."

She shook her head. "Not that. What's it printed on?"

I held it up. "Paper."

"And paper comes from..."

I narrowed my eyes, starting to see her intended

connection. "Trees," I said in a tone that I hoped told her I was not amused.

"And how do we harvest trees?"

She'd reverted to talking to me like I was one of her students. I folded my arms across my chest.

"By cutting them down," Isabelle piped up from the back seat.

I glanced at her from over my shoulder.

"And are you saying that they are celebrating..." She paused and glanced back at Isabelle. "C-h-r-i—"

"I get what you're saying."

"—every time they cut one down?"

I shot her a look. "No. Obviously not."

Clara's smile was triumphant as she nodded. "Right. They aren't. So we can do it, too." She slowed and took a right down the snow-covered gravel road. The Christmas tree farm loomed in the distance.

I sighed. She got me this time. "Fine. But we're not d-e-c-o-rating"—I got tired of spelling the word—"it."

I could tell that was not the answer Clara wanted, but she didn't argue, instead she just shrugged. "Fine."

I nodded. "Good." I was really curious if, by the end of the night, she was going to spin decorating the tree the same way. I couldn't imagine she'd be able to actually do that, but I wouldn't put it past her to try.

We shifted and moved with each dip and bump in the road. When we got to the parking lot, Clara found the closest spot to the entrance and took it. I sunk lower into my seat, grateful that we were a good thirty minutes from Grinchland. The last thing I needed was for someone from town to see me.

It would make for an awkward and strained meeting.

Isabelle was out of the car before I'd even unbuckled. Thankfully, Clara seemed just as eager and had joined her. They were standing next to one another, staring at me expectantly.

"There goes my hasty retreat," I muttered to myself as I pressed the tongue release and let the seat belt retract across my chest. I took my time finding the door handle. Just as I cracked the door, Isabelle was there to pull it open the rest of the way. "Thanks, Belly," I said half-heartedly.

"Come on, Daddy. You're taking for-ever." She placed her little hands on her hips and gave me a withering look.

"I'm sorry," I said as I climbed out of the car, stretching until Isabelle tried to shut the door but just ended up swinging it into me. The force took the wind out of my lungs, and I bent forward with a gasp.

"Thanks," I murmured.

"So why are we here?" Isabelle asked as she turned toward Clara. She rose up onto her tiptoes a few times. She was excited.

"We're here to cut down a tree."

Isabelle's eyes were wide. "Why?" she whispered.

I stepped out from behind the door so I could slam it closed. "Yeah, Ms. Snow. *Why* do you want to cut down a tree?"

Clara shot me an annoyed look before she squatted down in front of Isabelle so she was now eye level with my daughter. "To put in my house."

Isabelle laughed. "Why would you want a tree in your house?" She paused. "You don't have any dirt."

"Yeah, trees need dirt," I said, enjoying the chance to razz Clara.

Clara flicked her gaze up at me for a moment before she turned her attention back to Isabelle. "Because I think they are pretty and smell good. Lots of people have plants in their homes."

Isabelle stopped, and a thoughtful expression passed over her face. Then she began to nod slowly before she knit her eyebrows together. "But trees are bigger than flowers."

"True, but it's not impossible to put a tree in your house." She leaned forward, holding Isabelle's gaze. "What do you think? Do you think you can help me pick one out? I'm in desperate need of your expertise."

I waited to hear Isabelle's response. Finally she nodded. "I think I can do that."

I smiled and wrapped my arm around Isabelle's shoulders. "Lead the way, Ms. Snow."

We spent the next thirty minutes looking at trees that looked exactly the same, even though Clara tried to convince me that they were different. She kept going back and forth between a blue spruce and a Douglas fir. I was bored and antsy and trying really hard to feign interest, but my patience-meter for picking a non-Christmas Christmas tree was moments away from reaching max capacity.

Needing something to do, I grabbed Isabelle's hand. "I'm going to walk around with Belly," I said over my shoulder to Clara, who was in a heated discussion with the tree farm owner over the life expectancy of the two trees.

Thankfully, Isabelle didn't fight me. She settled her little hand into mine as we started walking down the aisle.

"It's weird, Daddy," she said as she swept her gaze around. "These trees were cut down. How's Ms. Snow going to plant them in her house?" She paused and pointed to the cleanly cut bottom of a Christmas tree.

"She can put it in a bucket of water to keep it for a bit longer, but it will eventually die." The last few words came out a whisper. I rarely talked about death. It felt like, in a way, I was talking about Nicole. I hated that death was a concept that was already an integral part of my daughter's life. Not addressing it felt immature, but I didn't know how to explain to my five-year-old daughter that her mother was never coming home in a way that she would understand, so I just avoided the topic altogether.

When I talked about Nicole, it broke me, so I just avoided it.

Isabelle's eyes were wide as she studied me. Then her little lip quivered. "So that tree is dying?" she asked as she pointed to the tree at the far end of the line. Its needles were already turning brown and its branches were sparse. It looked like it was placed there to be discarded later.

I wrapped my arms around Isabelle and hoisted her up. I pressed my lips to her cheek before I blew a raspberry in it. "You have such a kind heart," I said.

She giggled, but there was still a hint of sadness that told me she wasn't going to be so easily distracted. Thankfully, Clara appeared between the trees with a relieved smile on her lips.

"There you two are," she said as she started to walk toward us. "I've been looking for you."

For a moment, this whole situation felt right. Clara, looking for us, finding us, and then walking up to us like... we were together. I wondered if this was what it would feel like to be a little family, just the three of us.

I blinked, that thought taking me completely by surprise.

I wasn't spending time with Clara because I wanted to find a wife for me and a mother for Isabelle. I was with her because she was leaving in a few short months, and I wanted my life to go back to normal once she was gone—preferably before that if I won the wager.

I was spending time with Clara now so I didn't have to spend time with her in the future. Thinking about us as a family...that was never going to happen.

I forced myself from my thoughts and back to the present. Clara was glancing around, her cheeks flushed, and there was a sparkle to her eyes. "I just can't decide which one to get," she said as she blew out her breath.

Her gaze met mine for a moment. My thoughts of us as a family returned, and for some reason, they rendered me speechless. Clara knit her eyebrows together a moment before she turned her attention to Isabelle.

"What do you think?" She leaned in. "Which tree should I get?"

Isabelle was quiet for a moment before she pointed toward the dying one at the end of the row. "The one that doesn't have friends."

Clara looked confused as she followed Isabelle's gesture. "The one that doesn't have friends?" She glanced back at Isabelle first and then to me.

I bumped Isabelle a few times. She had such a tender heart and I loved her for it. "She's talking about the one that's dying." I nodded toward the brown tree.

Clara followed my motion and her expression softened as she stared at it. A soft smile spread across her lips as she glanced back at Isabelle.

"Is that the perfect one?" she asked.

Isabelle nodded. "I think so."

Clara paused. "I think so, too."

Once again, I was rendered speechless. I'd seen Clara's house. A half-dead Christmas tree was not part of her aesthetic. She lived and breathed the quintessential Christmas experience. Why was she agreeing to this tree?

"You don't have to get that one," I assured her.

She shook her head. "Nope. It's the perfect tree."

She didn't stop or look back as she marched off and reappeared with one of the employees who looked like he'd just turned eighteen. He had floppy brown hair and wore sunglasses and a name tag that read Taz.

"That one," she said as she pointed toward the tree that Isabelle had picked out.

Taz glanced at her like she was crazy. "That one's dead."

Clara shrugged. "We want it."

"It was going to be collected later today to head to the wood chipper."

Clara stared at him. "Are you saying I can't purchase this one?"

"No, I'm not saying that. I just..." He glanced back at me as if he were looking for backup.

I just shrugged. "It's what the ladies want." I could tell that Taz wanted to keep talking about this, but I just shook my head. This was a battle that he was not going to win.

"There's a no return policy if it...well, it's already dying, so there's a no return policy."

Clara shook her head. "That's fine. I don't have any intention of returning it," she said as she started rifling around in her purse and finally emerged with her wallet.

I couldn't help but stare at her, confusion coating my mind. I thought I'd had her pegged. She was just an overly zealous consumer who thought the meaning of this time of year was the amount of presents under her tree and the number of Christmas lights adorning her house. I thought she was Martha May Whovier.

But buying a dead tree that would stand out like a sore thumb against her other decorations was the opposite of who I thought Clara was. And I wasn't sure how I felt about this revelation.

Clara must have felt my stare because suddenly she looked up and locked her gaze with mine. She studied me for a moment before she drew her eyebrows together. "What?" she asked as she brought her hand to her cheek. "Do I have something on my face?"

I shook my head. "No."

She dropped her hand. "Then why are you staring at me like that?"

"You're confusing me," I confessed. As soon as the words were out, I wished I could take them back.

"I'm confusing you?" she repeated back to me.

I nodded. "I don't like it."

Clara didn't look apologetic or like she had any intention of giving up her annoying Christmas-ban-breaking ways. Instead she just frowned. "I'm sorry," she said in a tone that told me she really wasn't apologizing.

I bumped Isabelle a few times and she squealed. "Good, you should be," I said flicking my gaze to Clara, who was staring at me with sheer confusion.

"If you want to pull your car around, we can get you loaded up," Taz said as he handed Clara back her card.

Our conversation drifted to the back of my mind as we

focused on trying to get the tree tied to Clara's car. For a moment, I wanted to ask her why she didn't just let me drive, but then decided against it. With the tree now strapped to the roof, we climbed back inside and Clara drove off.

"Back home?" I asked.

Clara laughed as she took a left. "No. The day has only just begun."

SIXTEEN
CLARA

I celebrated a bit inside when Silas went along with my plot to pick out a Christmas tree. I honestly thought that he was going to put up a bigger fight. Granted, I'd come prepared with logical reasons as to why cutting down a tree didn't have to solely be a Christmas tradition. I could tell that he thought it was a stretch, but he didn't demand we leave, so I went ahead with it.

I was just as prepared for our second stop. After a quick Google search, I discovered that one of the best places to get hot chocolate in Maine was only twenty miles out from Grinchland. Cornerstone Cafe was in a small town called Lewisville. The reviews for this place were off the charts.

Silas looked confused as I pulled into the parking lot. When he opened the front door to the diner and saw the big sign that said, *Santa's Stamp of Approval: Best Hot Chocolate Ever*, he glanced over at me deadpan.

"Hey, all chocolate is liquid at some point. Are you saying that it's *all* Christmas related?" I was speaking the truth. "Besides, it's chocolate and it's hot. That's all."

He looked annoyed but didn't demand that we head back to my car and drive back to Grinchland. Instead, he ordered a water while Isabelle and I ordered something called Rudolph's Red Nose, which was a peppermint hot chocolate with a giant dollop of whip cream, Santa sprinkles, and a cherry on top. I ordered it sans the sprinkles because *that* would make it Christmas.

Isabelle and I giggled as we tried to outdo the other on how big of a whip cream mustache we could make. We made it to the tip of our noses and then spent the next few minutes with our eyes crossed, looking at them.

My gaze drifted over to Silas, who was sitting there with his glass of water and ice, watching us. His expression was unreadable, but he seemed content. When I offered him my cup of cocoa so he could join us, he wrinkled his nose and stated that he preferred his chocolate solid as opposed to a liquid.

I clapped my hands before I pointed to him and declared that he was getting it.

He was not amused.

Our next stop was in Kirkland, about twenty minutes to the east of Grinchland. I'd read online that there was an ice sculpture display that rivaled the Harbin International

Ice and Snow Sculpture Festival in China. I'd been wanting to go since I got to Grinchland but hadn't found the time. Today seemed like the perfect time.

The display was in downtown Kirkland. I heard Silas sigh as we drove by the sign that announced the Ice Sculpture Garden was ten miles away. I glanced over at him, but he was already looking at me expectantly. Like he was just waiting for me to come up with some ridiculous reason why he shouldn't be angry. How ice sculptures didn't have to be Christmas related.

And I did just that. As soon as we were parked and walking toward the entrance, I explained to him that ice sculptures were used for all kinds of things. Weddings. Dinner parties. Graduations. They were used on cruises. And none of those things screamed Christmas.

He kept his lips drawn into a tight line as he listened to me. He didn't believe me, but thankfully, he seemed to appreciate the effort I put into my reasoning.

I made sure to point out every ice sculpture that wasn't Christmas themed. The horse. The castle. The shirtless man with a scarf around his neck. That one had us both staring at it with our heads tipped back wondering who was the one that signed off on that proposal.

By the end of the display, Silas had joined in with me, making note of all the non-Christmas sculptures.

We were exhausted by the time we got back to my car. Since the town we were in was on the other side of Grinchland, we had forty minutes until we were back home. Isabelle promptly fell asleep in the back after being on the road for five minutes. That left Silas and me to drive in silence.

I kept peeking over at him, wondering what he was thinking. Was he mad at me? He didn't look mad. His expression was soft and his body language was relaxed. It was a night and day difference to how he reacted when I first met him on my porch.

But Silas's body language didn't always accurately depict his thoughts. Did he feel like I'd hoodwinked him into doing Christmas things with his daughter? I'd really tried to pick innocuous things for us to do. Ones that would check off my Christmas bucket list while reminding him why this time of year was special. My goal was still to get him to repeal his ban on Christmas, and I was determined to emerge triumphant at the end of these seven days.

I just wished there was a way of finding out if he was disappointed in me without asking point-blank.

"Tired?" I settled on an easy question to break the ice between us.

I could feel his gaze shift to me, but I decided to keep my focus on the road. He sighed. "Yeah." Then he glanced over his shoulder. "But not as tired as Belly." He paused, a soft smile spreading across his lips before he turned forward again.

"I hope it's a good tired," I said as I turned on my blinker and merged onto the highway. Once I was going the same speed as the other cars, I settled back in my seat.

"It's an okay tired."

An okay tired, I was okay with that. There was a lull as I tried to come up with something else to talk about.

"Is there a plan for tomorrow?"

His sudden question startled me, and I almost swallowed my tongue. I blinked, wondering if I'd heard his question right. When I glanced over, he was looking at me like he expected me to answer.

I'd heard right. It was just so startling because it didn't hold the same level of annoyance he'd had in the past.

"I have a few things planned…if you want." I still wasn't sure if he was serious or joking. I was waiting for him to yell, "Psych!" before telling me that there was no chance he'd ever want to spend time with me.

"I'm guessing it's 'not' Christmas related?" he asked, putting air quotes around the word *not*.

I wasn't sure if he was serious, so I decided to take it as a joke.

I smiled and winked. "Yep. It's *not* Christmas related."

He studied me, confusion coating his gaze. "So it's not Christmas related?"

Now I was getting confused as well. "No. I made you a promise that if it involves Isabelle, it won't be Christmas related." I glanced over at him. "I keep my promises."

He held my gaze before he nodded. "I believe you."

I turned my attention fully to the road so I could

process what had just happened. There were a few moments today, when I caught Silas watching me, that he didn't look disgusted or annoyed like he had in the past. Instead, he just looked...lost. Like he didn't know what to think.

I tried to write it off as boredom. After all, just because Isabelle and I were enjoying ourselves, it didn't mean Silas had the same enthusiasm. But then he'd say something, or do something, and I'd wonder if maybe I was getting through to him.

I wished I knew what had happened in his past for him to cancel Christmas. He seemed to tolerate my justifications for why today's activities weren't Christmas specific—even though I knew he thought it was ridiculous—so he had some level of acceptance for the holiday.

Without knowing the real reason, I felt like I was shooting in the dark. Trying to make two pieces come together when I couldn't figure out the path to get them there.

As the principal, Maria had to know. She seemed like the perfect person to ask. Monday morning I was going to march right into her office and refuse to leave until she told me.

But there was a day and a half until school resumed, and I still had tomorrow's festivities to get through. I'd plan something from my Christmas bucket list and hope it wasn't the thing that would send Silas into a spiral where he'd call off this entire bet and walk away.

I started to slow when I got to his house. Just before I turned into his driveway, he spoke.

"I'll help you unload your tree," he said as he motioned to the roof of my car.

Right. The tree. "Um, okay," I said as I picked up speed a bit so I could pull into my driveway. I kept my car running to keep Isabelle warm as we both climbed out and removed the straps that were holding the tree down.

Once it was loose, he pulled it down in one swift movement. I wasn't sure what to do to help, so I settled on hurrying ahead of him so I could get the door. When we were both inside, I motioned toward the living room, where I'd set out a stand this morning.

Silas paused. "Are you sure you want this tree in your front window?" he asked. I thought he was going to remind me of the city ordinances that I would break. Instead, he glanced around. "It doesn't really go with everything else."

I did a quick once-over of the living room but came up with a completely different conclusion. "I think it fits perfectly with everything in this room."

Sure, on the outside, it appeared that I had a certain aesthetic, but the truth was, if you looked closer, it had less to do with how things *looked* and more about how they made me *feel*. Everything in this room had meaning to me. Everything held memories that I feared I would forget if I ever let them go.

Picking out this tree with Isabelle was a memory I was going to cherish forever, even if she believed the reason we picked the tree was mundane. I would never forget how she asked me to buy the tree that had no friends. It showed her sweet heart and caring demeanor. It reminded me of what was important and to not overlook that in favor of perfection.

But I doubted Silas would understand that.

"It's perfect," I said as I centered the tree stand in the middle of the window and then stepped back so Silas could hoist the trunk up and into the hole. Once it was straight, I knelt down and cinched the nuts to keep the tree upright.

Silas lingered for a moment, and I wondered if it was because he was waiting for me to change my mind. I found a nearby pair of scissors that we'd used last night for popcorn string and cut the netting around the tree.

Silas declared that he was going to head out. I was distracted with wrapping the tree with lights, so I just told him goodbye as he walked back to the front door and left. He carried Isabelle past the window as he made his way to his house.

Remembering that I'd left my car running, I set the lights down and hurried outside to turn it off. When I got back inside, I focused my attention on placing the lights perfectly on each branch before I shifted to hanging the popcorn garland. Once the tree was decorated to my satisfaction, my stomach growled, so I plugged the lights in and headed into the kitchen to reheat the soup I'd made last night.

With my spoon and bowl in hand, I made my way back to the living room to curl up on the couch and enjoy the ambiance of the Christmas lights. The sun had disappeared beyond the horizon and darkness had coated the room. Just as I tucked my right foot under me and moved to sit, someone in Silas's front yard caught my attention.

I kept myself upright as I peered through the window to get a better look. It seemed as if Silas was in his yard, hammering something into the snow-covered ground. I moved closer to the window to get a better look. In the light from my decorations mixed with the street lights, it looked like he was prepping Pudgie.

A smile emerged. He'd kept his word.

I took a few bites of my soup while I watched him finish staking the penguin. Then he headed back to his garage and out of my view. I wondered if he was going to actually turn it on—after all, that hadn't been part of our agreement—but he returned with what looked like a wooden sign with him.

He pounded it into the ground next to where Pudgie was lying. Then, he moved to the front where he leaned from side to side like he was trying to assess if that was the right place to put it.

The way my eyes were glued to Silas, I felt like I was watching a murder mystery. I'd set my forgotten soup on the armrest behind me so I could fully focus.

Silas finally nodded, gathered his tools, and disappeared back into his garage. When he didn't come back out, I settled in on the couch to finish my now cold soup.

I was humming to the Christmas music playing on my phone when, suddenly, Pudgie started to inflate. It was like watching the living dead rise up from the grave. I returned to my post by the window to see if I could get the full effect of the inflatable plus whatever Silas had added.

After craning my neck to get a better look, I could finally see what it was.

Written in black paint on a piece of plywood was the word, "Seriously?" with an arrow pointing to my house.

SEVENTEEN
SILAS

I was surprised when I woke up the next morning in a good mood. It was almost as if I was actually excited to see what Clara had planned for us today. Most weekends, I spent the time cleaning and grocery shopping—all in an effort to keep myself from wallowing. But with Clara around, I didn't have the time.

She was the distraction that I hadn't realized I needed.

Clara texted me last night, letting me know she was going to be at my house around one. She told me to dress warm because we were going to be outside. Normally, I didn't like surprises and wanted to be informed on everything, but I knew she wasn't going to tell me even if I asked, so I just sent a thumbs-up emoji and left it at that.

Isabelle and I filled the morning doing laundry, playing with Barbies, and having an impromptu dance party in the living room. We'd just finished lunch when there was a knock on the front door.

Excitement rose up inside of me, but I managed to shove it down enough to give Isabelle a stern look that I hoped said, *What did I say about answering the door?* and then headed into the foyer to let Clara in.

She was mid knock when I pulled the door open. Her eyes were wide as her gaze met mine. It was almost as if she was not prepared to have me answer the door. Our gazes locked, and for a moment, neither of us looked away.

Then, as if she realized what was going on between us, she dropped her gaze to her feet before she turned and looked over her shoulder. "I didn't think you'd actually do it," she said, waving toward her penguin that I'd set up last night.

I shrugged, folded my arms, and leaned against the doorframe, all the while keeping my gaze focused on Clara. There was something about her. Something had shifted between us. Did she feel it too? Or was I the only idiot that was losing his grasp on what our deal had been all along.

"What can I say? I'm a man of my word." I paused. "But I did make it my own."

Clara glanced back at me. "I saw the sign."

I gave her a wicked half smile. "Can't have Grinchland residents thinking that I'm going soft. This way, it portrays exactly what is happening."

She quirked an eyebrow. "And what is happening?"

I leaned in, enjoying the surge of electricity that crackled between our bodies. It had been a long time since I'd been this close to a woman. Normally, I would instantly pull back, but I didn't. Instead, I allowed myself to linger. To enjoy.

Realizing that she was waiting for my response, I whispered, "You're twisting my arm." I took in a deep breath and with it the smell of her shampoo. It had the scent of sweet vanilla and reminded me of my grandmother baking Christmas cookies when I was a kid.

I blinked and pulled back, startled by the sudden resurfacing of that memory. It had been a long time since I'd thought about any of my past Christmases except for the one I was always actively trying to forget.

"Oh," was all she could respond before Isabelle appeared and whisked Clara away to show off her collection of dresses that quickly turned into an all-out fashion show.

They were elbow deep in satin and taffeta when I asked Clara what the afternoon plan was. She suddenly snapped to attention like she was just remembering why she was here and that we had a schedule.

She promised a disappointed Isabelle that she would be back for the second half of the production, and explained that if we didn't leave now, we'd miss out. On what, she didn't expound, and when I asked, she just flashed me a smile and told me that I'd have to wait and see. A response that I was growing accustomed to despite my better judgement.

At least I convinced her to let us take my truck this time. She eyed me cautiously before she jutted out her pinkie finger and made me promise right then and there that I was going to follow her directions religiously.

I locked pinkies with her, looked her dead in the eye, and repeated that I would follow her directions religiously. I tried to ignore the sensations that raced up my arm from the feel of her skin against mine. She paused, taking her time to really study me before she nodded and told me I could drive.

It was a pleasant drive until her directions led us to Kingston, a small town about thirty minutes from Grinchland. I was confused as to what we were going to do there as I pulled onto Main Street. It wasn't until she guided me to their city park that I realized her plan.

"Ice skating?" I asked as I obeyed her instructions to turn left into the parking lot.

"Ice skating," she repeated as she looked over at me. "Have you ever gone?"

I turned off the engine and pulled my keys from the ignition. "Once when I was ten. My pops wanted me to be the next Wayne Gretzky, but the moment I got on the ice, I fell on my butt. That was the end of my career."

Those words made me pause. This was the second time today that holiday memories from my childhood had resurfaced. First with the smell of Clara's shampoo and now this. I actively tried not to be a sentimental person, and yet here I was, practically skipping down memory lane.

Her eyebrows were knit together and I chuckled. She could list every reindeer that pulled Santa's sleigh, but she didn't know who Wayne Gretzky was.

"Famous hockey player."

Her lips parted into an O. "Well, let's see how it goes this time." As she passed by me, she bumped me with her shoulder. "Maybe we'll discover your true calling in life."

I stared at her as she wrapped her hand around Isabelle's and they walked together toward the entrance of the skating rink. I wasn't sure if it was from the sensation of her shoulder on mine or the motherly way she looked down at my daughter with wide eyes and full attention, but my entire body felt frozen in time. Like this was a moment I never wanted to forget.

An ache of sadness rushed through my chest. This was a moment Nicole would never get to have with her daughter. I waited for the pain and grief that always followed thoughts of Nicole, but they never came. Instead, this sense of peace settled around me. It was as if Nicole were here, witnessing what was transpiring between our daughter and Clara. And for some strange reason, it felt like this had been her plan all along.

Almost as if...she'd sent Clara to us.

"Daddy!"

Isabelle's voice snapped me from my trance. I blinked,

trying to clear my mind and focus on the present. I combed through the crowd of people until I found my daughter. She was standing at the ticket booth with Clara, and they were both staring at me expectantly. I didn't want either to ask me if I was okay, so I nodded and hurried to join them.

After our tickets were purchased and we were through the turnstile, Clara took both our shoe sizes and hurried off to rent some skates. I followed Isabelle to the rink, where she rose up onto her tiptoes so she could see over the barrier. Her eyes locked on a group of girls who were dressed in sequin leotards and tulle skirts. They were engaged in some synchronized skating.

I'd never seen my daughter's eyes so wide.

"Daddy," she whispered as her hand found my forearm and she began to shake it. "Daddy," she whispered again, never pulling her gaze from the girls. "Daddy!" she said, more desperate the third time.

I crouched down so I was eye level with her. "What?" I asked.

"Do you see them? Do you see the princesses?" she asked as she pointed her little forefinger in their direction.

"Princesses? Where?" I asked, my tone turned teasing.

"There," she said, exasperated. How could I *not* see what she was seeing.

"I'm not sure..."

Her gaze snapped to mine and her eyes widened like

she was daring me to say I couldn't see them. I chuckled and held up my hands. "I see them. I see them," I said.

That seemed to satisfy her as she turned her attention back to the girls. I realized that there was no way I could compete with princesses on skates, so I sat down on the bench next to her and leaned forward, resting my elbows on my knees as I let my mind wander.

What had that been earlier? It had been months since I'd felt Nicole's presence. There was a time I'd feared I was going to forget her altogether. I poured myself into our daughter and Grinchland. But today, while watching Clara and Isabelle, I felt her again.

I felt her peace. It was something that I'd missed and longed for.

"I've got them," Clara sang out.

I glanced over to see her with three sets of ice skates slung over her shoulder. Her cheeks were flushed and her eyes glistened when she caught my gaze. My stomach lightened at the sight of her. It was in stark contrast to how I reacted during our first few interactions.

I shook my head. I needed to get my mind right. We were here to stop Clara from talking to the town council. We were here to stop her from "saving" Christmas. My mission was simple: survive the full seven days and then watch her walk away from Grinchland with my bylaws still intact.

I was doing this so everything could return to normal.

We put on our ice skates, and as soon as I stood, I

knew I'd made a mistake. My ankle just about gave out as I stood on the thin blades. Whoever thought that pushing yourself around ice on a tiny piece of metal was a good idea should have their head examined.

Clara held both of Isabelle's hands as she helped her to the rink. I wanted to call Clara back and ask her to help me as well, but I decided against it. It was better to figure this out on my own than admit that I was not cut out for it.

Thankfully, in four long steps I was to the barrier. I tried to hide how hard I was clinging to it as I gingerly stepped out onto the ice. Clara had left Isabelle in search of a walker for her to use. When she came back, I wanted to ask for one for me, but I decided against it. Instead, I hung onto Isabelle's walker for dear life, much to her chagrin.

"Daddy," she complained as she shook the walker in an attempt to free herself from me. "Daddy."

I ignored her. There was no way I was going to let go. I knew as soon as I did, my feet would slip out from under me and I'd slam into the ice. When I was a kid, I had no problem bouncing back. But as a thirty-year-old man, I was sure something was bound to break.

"Everything okay?" Clara asked. When I glanced up, I could see that her question was directed to me, not Isabelle.

"Yeah, yeah," I said, glancing down at my daughter. "She's getting the hang of it." I forced a smile as I turned my attention back to Clara.

She quirked an eyebrow. "Really?"

"Daddy, you need to let go," Isabelle said, more forceful this time. Her face was scrunched up in annoyance as she stared up at me. I could tell that she wanted to take off, but my weight was holding her back.

"Here," Clara said with a soft chuckle. She extended her hand and wiggled her fingers. "I'll help your daddy stay upright so you can go."

I stared at her hand, knowing what it meant, but unable to actually take it. I tried to tell her no, but she just sighed and rested her hand on my left one.

"Come on. I don't bite."

"Yeah, Daddy. Ms. Snow's got you." Isabelle was trying to be patient, but I could hear it waning in the tone of her voice.

I wanted to reject Clara's invitation. I wanted to tell her that I was fine. That Isabelle was fine. But I also didn't want to keep holding my daughter back. Ice skating might not be my true calling, but it could be Isabelle's, and who was I to keep that dream from her.

Just as I straightened, taking my weight off the walker, Isabelle took that as her sign to get moving. She pushed forward. And in an effort to keep myself upright, I scrambled to grab Clara's hand. She held me up as I got my feet under me and my weight distributed. Our hands were clasped and she was staring up at me as if to ask if I was okay.

"I'm good, I'm good," I said at the same time my feet

began to shift, and I had to scramble to keep them under me again.

"Maybe ice skating isn't your calling," Clara said. The strain of keeping me upright was evident in her voice.

I started to tell her that I was more than happy to wait off the ice, but she just motioned with her head toward the rink that stretched out in front of us.

"Come on. It's the standing still that'll get you. It's best to keep moving."

With my hand in hers, she started to skate. I tried to follow her lead. I tried to match her rhythm as she pushed her skates forward, but I was struggling. I was waiting for her to call it quits, but those words never came. Instead, she just offered me words of encouragement as we slowly crossed the ice.

On the second trip around the rink, I glanced over at her. I was more confident, even though I was far from the smooth glide that seemed to come naturally to everyone else. When Isabelle passed by us and I saw the look of pure joy on her face, the desire to thank Clara rose up inside of me, and there was no way I was going to be able to keep it in much longer.

Even though Clara and I were opposites when it came to Christmas, I couldn't deny that spending time with her had been good for Isabelle. And when it came to my daughter, nothing mattered more to me.

"Thanks," I said, my voice low and filled with emotion that startled even me.

Clara glanced over. "For what?"

I paused, taking a moment to gather my thoughts. I wanted to be specific. While I was grateful for her introducing my daughter to new things, that didn't carry over to Clara's flagrant disregard for the no-Christmas laws in Grinchland.

"I guess I always saw winter activities as steeped in Christmas, but you helped me see that I was wrong. I've kept my daughter away from things that she so obviously adores." I nodded toward Isabelle, who was a few feet off. She'd stopped to admire the dancing princesses as they moved past her.

When Clara didn't answer right away, I glanced over to see that her expression had stilled and she looked deep in thought. Had she heard me?

"Clara?" I asked.

Her gaze snapped to mine and a smile emerged. A smile that quickened my heart rate. I inwardly shushed it because that was not what I was here to do.

"You're welcome," she said, her voice soft as she gently squeezed my hand. "Although, I really do think you should give Christmas another chance. I'm of the belief that steeping activities in Christmas spirit actually makes things better, not worse."

I raised an eyebrow. This I had to hear. "Is that so? Can you give me an example?"

Clara dropped her gaze as a thoughtful expression emerged. Then she smiled back up at me. "Christmas cookies. Christmas trees. Christmas ice sculptures." She sighed. "They even just sound better."

I frowned. "That's only three things."

"Christmas music. Christmas lights. Christmas movies." She paused before she shrugged. "Even kisses."

Heat pricked at the back of my neck. I whipped my gaze to meet hers, wondering where she was going with this. "Kisses?" I asked before I could stop myself. I knew I shouldn't encourage her, not when my body temperature was rising to a heat that could melt this entire rink. But I was curious. The other six examples I understood, but *kisses*? I had to hear this.

Clara glanced over at me with a shy smile. "Haven't you ever had a mistletoe kiss?"

"A mistletoe kiss?"

She nodded. "It's like a kissing booth, but better. The anticipation. The waiting. Wondering if the person you want to kiss will take the opportunity to meet you under the mistletoe." She shrugged. "It's like nothing you'll ever experience."

I really didn't know what to say to that other than, "Huh." I'd never shared a mistletoe kiss, and I wasn't sure how much longer I could stand here and listen to her talk about what it was like to experience one.

I was a man after all.

Clara shrugged. "Don't knock it until you try it."

Thankfully, Isabelle caught up with us, and Clara went from talking about mistletoe kisses to praising my daughter. They decided that it was best to leave me waiting along the wall so the two of them could go off together. *I* was the unwanted weight that was holding them back.

Once I had something sturdy to hold onto, I half skated–half walked my way back to the opening of the rink and out onto the rubber flooring. As soon as I got to the bench, I collapsed on it. I couldn't take the skates off fast enough, and I exhaled with pure joy once my shoes were back on and I could stand without the fear of falling over.

I returned my skates to the rental counter and spent the rest of the time watching Clara coach my daughter. Isabelle gained confidence, and every so often she let go of the walker and took a few glides forward unassisted.

She was a chatterbox all the way home. I sat back in the driver's seat, my hand resting on the steering wheel as I listened to Clara engage her in conversation. Isabelle was determined to come back here to practice, and I was not allowed to say no.

I just smiled as I stared at the road in front of me. If only Isabelle knew that saying no to her was impossible. I'd seen the spark in her eyes. If she wanted to become an ice skater, I was not in the business of standing in the way of her dreams.

I pulled into Clara's driveway to drop her off. She pulled on the door release and hopped down to the ground. Just as she turned to shut the door, she paused and glanced up at me.

"I had fun," she said, her gaze turning shy as she studied me.

I knew I should tell her that I hated it. I knew I should tell her to never take us to a place like that again. I knew I should have just kept quiet.

Instead, I offered her a genuine smile and said, "Me, too."

EIGHTEEN
CLARA

I was too jittery to go to bed. After Silas dropped me off, I showered and got dressed in my Santa-falling-down-a-chimney pajamas and got started making hot potato casserole—a Gran tradition after ice skating. With a full stomach and the softest pajamas known to man, I should have felt ready to snuggle up on the couch under my *this is my Hallmark watching blanket* blanket, and fall asleep to *A Christmas Story*, but no matter how hard I tried, I had too much energy.

Maybe it was just adrenaline from ice skating. Or maybe it was the anticipation for the new week of teaching. And maybe—this was probably the most likely—something had shifted between Silas and me.

I'd gone from thinking he loathed my guts to thinking he only mildly hated my guts. That was progress.

In desperate need of a distraction from these ridiculous thoughts, I decided the best course of action was to pour my energy into decorating Isabelle's tree with ornaments. I took my time picking the perfect ones from the box I'd saved and only hung the most valuable ones on the branches. The ones that I cherished.

After I finished decorating, I took a step back. The tree was perfect, but there was something wrong. It didn't look right. I tipped my head to the side. Maybe if I looked at it from a different angle, I'd figure out what wasn't working.

"It's Santa," I said as I stepped forward and grabbed the three-foot Santa figurine I'd placed next to the window the other day. I moved him to the other side of the room and then turned to see if that solved the issue.

Something was still wrong.

I gathered the five Christmas gift boxes that were wrapped in plaid fabric and progressively got smaller, and I moved them over to where I'd put Santa. The three-foot nutcracker was next. Then the sleigh full of pinecones. I didn't stop until the only thing that remained in the middle of that wall was the Christmas tree.

I stared at it, tapping my chin. Was that it? Was that the issue? I closed my eyes and a sense of calm and peace passed over me. I took in a deep breath as I opened them again. Even though this was the first time I'd ever left a wall this bare in my life, it was...perfect.

I settled down on the couch and pulled my blanket over my lap. I turned on the TV and found *A Christmas Story* and snuggled deeper into the cushions.

I was halfway through the movie when my phone rang. It blared "I Want a Hippopotamus for Christmas"—Abbie's ringtone,

"Hey," I said as I pressed the green talk button and brought my phone to my cheek.

"Hey, friend! Just checking in to make sure you're still alive."

I smiled as I leaned back against the couch again. "I'm alive."

"How's things going with the Grinch?"

My gaze drifted over to Silas's house. The penguin he'd agreed to put up in his front yard was still there with the ridiculous sign that he'd added. The lights from the inside shone in the darkness. Where it once looked sad and dark, it had begun to feel homey—despite the lack of other decorations.

What was happening to me?

"He's good. I'm good. We're good," I said as I pulled my attention from the window and stared at the paused movie on the screen.

"You're good?" Abbie asked. "You're living in a place that has outlawed Christmas, and you're...good?"

"Well, not that. I just don't...mind as much anymore."

When Abbie didn't respond right away, I realized that I'd made a mistake. She was never going to let me live this down.

"Do you have a fever? Take your temperature."

I sighed.

"Have you been kidnapped? Hurry, what's your favorite Christmas movie of all time?"

I drummed my fingers on my thighs as I waited for her to finish. When there was a lull, I started to ask her if she was done yet, but she wasn't. She had two more sets of questions to make sure that I hadn't joined a cult and I hadn't lost a bet. Once she was satisfied, she continued. "I think it's a good thing. You're participating in a sort of detox."

I frowned. "I may not care as much that the mayor doesn't like Christmas, but that doesn't mean I'm finished with it." I decided to keep my little spinout with the decorations around the tree in the living room to myself. No need to add fuel to Abbie's flames. I could only imagine her reasoning as to why fewer decorations were better.

"Well, it's a start." Then she paused. "Maybe that's what Grinchland can be. A place where the most Christmas crazed among us can go to rehab!"

"Okay, Abbie," I said, knowing she couldn't see I was rolling my eyes, but making sure that she'd understand the tone of my voice.

"My name is Clara, and I am addicted to Christmas," she joked.

"I'm hanging up now," I said, pulling the phone from my cheek and letting my thumb hover over the big red button.

"I love you, friend!" Abbie called out in a singsong voice.

"Love you, too, friend," I said as I hung up.

I set my phone down next to me on the couch and stared at it, Abbie's words repeating in my mind. There was a truth to what she said. When I was in Winter Springs, Christmas was my life. I lived and breathed the holiday. But here, in Grinchland, I was forced to step out of my traditions and look around. I was forced to see things differently. I was forced to see things not through Christmas lights and decorations, but to notice the simple parts of the holiday.

I was forced to enjoy the smallest of Christmas moments.

I shook my head, feeling crazy for letting myself digest Abbie's theories to this degree. Christmas was Christmas, and I'd always participated in the holiday just like everyone else.

I didn't need Christmas rehab, and I certainly didn't need to detox.

Abbie's words still plagued my mind when I woke up the next morning, but I did my best to push them from my mind. I had a day's worth of teaching followed by the next holiday-themed activity with Silas, so I needed to get my head on straight and focus.

I dressed and was out the door a little earlier this morning. I told myself it was because I was trying to be a better employee—getting to the school early instead of right on time—but deep down, I knew the real reason.

I just wasn't ready to admit that reason out loud.

I was sitting at my desk as students started to filter in. I'd kept my door propped open, and I justified that decision by telling myself that it made my room look more inviting. I wanted every student to feel like my door was open both physically and emotionally.

"Hey, Mayor."

The greeting made its way into my room, and my heart picked up speed as I moved to stand. There was no other reason I walked across my classroom and out the door—I wanted to see Silas.

He was standing in the hallway with Isabelle by his side. He was trying to get her to give him a hug, but Isabelle wasn't having it. As soon as he saw me, he straightened, his expression soft as he met my gaze.

"Hey," I said, my voice all hushed and shy. I inwardly cursed myself for being so transparent.

He didn't give me a full smile. Instead, it was this half smile that took my breath away. "Hey," he said.

I held his gaze a little longer until I started to scream at myself that if I didn't stop staring, he was going to suspect that something was wrong with me. And even though something *was* most definitely wrong with me, I wanted to keep that a secret for as long as I could.

"Are there any plans for tonight?" he asked. There was a hopeful hint to his voice that threw me off.

"Um, I'm not sure." And that was the truth. I'd spent the whole morning trying not to think about Silas, so I hadn't allowed myself to think of activities for us to do.

He nodded. "Let me know."

"Of course."

"Daddy, it's time for you to go," Isabelle said as she reached up and grabbed her backpack, which was slung on his shoulder.

He glanced down at her and then back up at me. "This will never get easy," he said as he allowed her to pull her backpack down and shove it into her locker.

"I bet."

Isabelle didn't wait for me to guide her into the room, and seconds later, it was just the two of us in the hallway. I knew I should tell him goodbye and head into the classroom, but I wanted to linger just a few moments longer.

And I allowed myself to think that Silas wanted the same.

"I'll text you the game plan," I hurried to say, hoping he believed I wanted to stay in the hall because of our challenge and not because I liked spending time with him —as strange as that was to admit.

"Sounds good." He paused. "I should go."

I nodded and motioned toward the classroom behind me. "Me, too."

He started to turn before he glanced back over his shoulder. "See you tonight, Clara."

My heart took off racing. This was the first time I'd heard him say my name. It was more exhilarating than I thought humanly possible.

"See you tonight, Silas," I whispered.

He smiled at me one more time and then made his way down the hall. I didn't mean to, but I stood there, watching him leave, until he'd turned the corner and disappeared.

I covered my face with both hands and then blew out my breath.

Whatever that had been was dangerous.

There was no way I could allow myself to fall for the Grinch of Grinchland. We were exact opposites. He was water and I was oil. He was ice and I was fire. And yet, right here, right now, none of that mattered.

Right now, all I wanted was to see him again.

THANKFULLY, a classroom full of wild kindergarteners kept me distracted for the rest of the day. There must have been a full moon, because everyone was off. Even my most even-keeled student was acting out. I tried to keep it together, but when Isaac snapped at Heather during art class, I folded my arms and told everyone that we needed a reset because they were all acting like Scrooge.

Melanie frowned as she raised her hand. "We're acting like a screw?" she asked.

I blinked at her question. "No, not a screw, Scrooge." I glanced around at my students, who all had the same blank stares. "Scrooge? Ebenezer Scrooge?" That did nothing to jog their memory. They were all just staring at me like I was crazy.

"It's from A Chr—" I stopped myself. "A Carol," I said in an effort to redeem myself.

And then I realized what was going on. These kids had been toddlers when Christmas was banned in Grinchland. There was a reason most of them had no idea what I was talking about, and that reason was Silas.

And then the best idea ever dawned on me.

I waited until all the kids were settled with painting sunsets to slip away to my desk to construct an email. It was short and sweet, and I included every parent plus Maria—I just kept Silas out. He was going to help me.

Dear kindergarten families,

I am planning to put on a play this week with the students. We will be doing A (blank) Carol. I will be finding ways to shorten it due to the time constraints. Please help your students with their parts, and I look forward to seeing you on Thursday for opening (and closing) night.

Ms. Snow

It only took two minutes after sending out the email for Maria to knock on my door. Her eyes were wide as she met my gaze for a moment. And then she turned her attention to the kids, smiling at them as she hurried to my desk.

"What is going on?" she asked, her voice hushed but pointed.

"It's fine," I said.

She frowned. "I told you not to involve the school. Silas is serious when it comes to Christmas."

"That's why I'm calling it *A Carol*. I think the story can stand on its own without mentioning Christmas."

Maria's eyes just got wider.

I sighed. "I mentioned Scrooge to the kids, and no one knew what I was talking about." I held up my hands. "Where I come from that is borderline criminal."

"But, Clara—"

"I have immunity." I folded my arms and met her gaze head-on.

She drew her eyebrows together. "You have what?"

"Immunity." I narrowed my eyes. "For about four more days. It's a deal I made with the mayor." I gave her a smile. "So don't worry, everything will be fine."

Her lips pursed and her nostrils flared, but I could tell that there was a part of her that was interested in seeing how this was all going to play out. When she sighed, I celebrated.

"You tell Silas that this was not my idea and that I tried to stop you, okay?"

I raised my right hand at a ninety-degree angle. "Will do."

She studied me for a moment longer before she sighed again and shook her head. "It's your funeral."

There was a part of me that wished she left the classroom on a more positive note. A "break a leg" would have been nice, but she just shook her head once more before heading out of the room.

Now alone, I glanced around before I picked up my phone and shot a quick text to Silas. He was going to be my little elf.

> Meet me at the elementary gymnasium tonight. I have a plan.

NINETEEN
SILAS

Clara spent the entire day sending me cryptic messages.

First, she told me to meet her at the elementary school gymnasium. Then she asked me to pick up a gallon of black paint and brushes. Then she asked me to pick up twinkle lights. To say I was sufficiently confused when I climbed into my truck after a quick trip to the hardware store was an understatement.

Thankfully, after I fed Isabelle dinner, Mrs. Bloomburg was more than happy to come over to help her get ready for bed. I told her I'd be back by nine at the latest, but she just shook her head and told me to take my time. As I walked out the door, she told me that she was happy to see me "get out there, again."

I wanted to turn around and tell her that I was being forced into leaving my house, that this wasn't voluntary, but I stopped myself. I knew she would just smile and say, "okay," but not really believe me. The best thing for me to do was to just leave it alone as I shut the door behind me and hurried to my truck.

It was seven thirty when I pulled into the elementary school parking lot. I let the engine idle for a moment before I turned it off and pulled the key from the ignition. I gathered the supplies Clara asked me to pick up and got out of my truck. The door to the cafeteria was unlocked, so I pulled it open and headed inside.

As I neared the gym, I heard voices. I frowned as I peeked through the door to see Clara and...Todd standing there. Todd was talking and Clara was nodding while she swept her gaze over the large pieces of plywood spread out on the floor in front of them.

Of all the things I thought we were going to do, being the third wheel to whatever was going on never crossed my mind. I was so confused as I stared at Todd. He hadn't mentioned coming here when I left the office a few hours ago...why hadn't he said anything?

The longer I watched them, the deeper my frown got. Clara looked so happy standing there with her hands clasped and with the biggest smile on her face. Todd was matching her energy as he moved his hands around while talking.

Clara never looked that happy to see me. She'd never looked so animated during our conversations. A surge of jealousy rushed through me. I blinked, not expecting that reaction at all. I shook my head, forcing that feeling from my mind.

I'd officially gone crazy.

Todd was the first person to notice my entrance. As soon as his gaze locked with mine, he grew quiet. That seemed to draw Clara's curiosity. When she saw me, her smile changed. It wasn't bad, but it wasn't the same as the one she'd given Todd. I was unsure of what that meant, and I knew, for my sanity, the last thing I should do was stand here and try to figure it out. So I cleared my throat and approached them.

"What's going on here?" I asked as I swept my gaze over the plywood.

"You're here!" Clara said as she clapped her hands. Her gaze dipped down to the bags I was carrying. "And you brought the stuff I asked you to bring." She glanced up at me and her smile emerged, causing my heart to inexplicably pound, again.

"Paint and twinkle lights," I said as I raised the bags slightly. Then I glanced over at Todd. "What are you doing here?" I winced. My tone had a bite to it that I hadn't intended.

This was all Clara's fault. She was confusing me and I hated that.

"Did you know that Todd is a master carpenter?" Clara asked, her wide smile had returned as her attention shifted back to Todd. "Look at what he created from just a few short text messages."

I glanced at the items that Clara was motioning toward. I wanted to be impressed, but I had no clue what they were or what I had to do with what was going on here. If Todd was her knight in shining armor, why did she call me?

I kept looking for a hint as to why I was here, but nothing came. I was standing here, clueless.

But Clara looked hopeful that I would be just as impressed as she was. Even though I wasn't sure how I felt about giving Todd so much praise, I could tell she wanted me to have a similar reaction, so I just smiled and nodded. "Looks great, Todd." Then I glanced back over to Clara. "I guess I'll leave the two of you to it." I set the bags down on the ground and turned to leave.

I didn't like feeling jealous. I didn't like that I'd interrupted what seemed like a date between the two of them. Why was I even here? Couldn't she have just had Todd pick up the paint and twinkle lights? It was strange that she would ask me to do it when they were perfectly capable of accomplishing the task.

"Where are you going?"

Clara's voice stopped me in my tracks. I paused, hating that I loved that she hadn't let me walk out of the gym, that for some reason, she wanted me to stay. Because, deep down, I wanted to stay with her. I didn't want to walk out and go back home.

"I'm going home," I said.

Clara's eyes widened. "Oh, okay," she said, doing nothing to mask the disappointment in her voice.

It got my heart racing. Did she want me to stay?

"Unless you need me for"—I circled my hand toward the plywood in front of me—"whatever this is."

Clara glanced from the plywood over to me. "I was kind of hoping that you could help me." Her expression turned shy as she glanced up at me.

Todd cleared his throat. "I think I'll head out. If you need anything, don't hesitate to ask." Clara thanked him, and then Todd turned his attention to me. "See you tomorrow, boss," he said.

I nodded.

Soon, Clara and I were alone in the gym. I wasn't sure what to say or where to look, so I settled on just staring at the floor. Thankfully, Clara took over and led the conversation.

"Are you okay with staying?" She held up her hands. "If you can't, I totally understand."

"Do you want me to stay?" Call me crazy, but I needed her to say yes. I needed to know that I wasn't the only one who felt our relationship changing. I'd gone from having to spend time with her...to wanting to spend time with her.

And I wanted her to admit that she wanted to spend time with me too.

Clara held my gaze as silence fell between us. Then she started to nod. "I want you to stay."

Slowly, ever so slowly, a smile began to spread across my lips. I shoved my hands into the front pockets of my jeans before I shrugged. "Then I'll stay."

"Okay." Clara's voice was soft and her gaze was shy.

I loved that when she was nervous her cheeks flushed and her eyes twinkled. Clara may be obsessed with Christmas lights, but I was obsessed with the glow that naturally flowed from her gaze. It was unlike anything man-made.

Needing to break the connection between us before I did something stupid, I pulled my gaze from hers and turned toward the wood that was lying on the ground. Our relationship had gone from antagonistic to tolerable. Making a stupid move now would ruin everything.

"What's the plan with all of this?" I asked as I glanced over at her.

Clara clapped her hands together, steepled her pointer fingers, and turned to face me. "We're putting on a play," she said, her voice reverent.

"A play?"

She nodded. "A *blank* Carol."

I frowned. "A blank Carol?"

She held my gaze. "You know, A c-h-r-i...A *blank* Carol." She moved her hand in a forward circle as if that was going to help me get there faster.

"The story of Scrooge?" I asked.

She nodded. "There you go! Now you're getting it."

"But when is the performance?"

"Thursday."

I balked. "Thursday? That's, like, three days away."

She blew out her breath. "I know. That's why we've got to start now." She walked over to the bags I'd brought and started rifling around.

"How are you going to make this Christmas play...not Christmas?"

Clara glanced up at me. "At its heart, it's a story about a grumpy man who has his heart changed by his past, present, and future." She emerged from the bag triumphantly with a brush in hand. "It's a tale as old as time," she said as she waved the brush in my direction. "Christmastime and the end of the year gives everyone the perfect opportunity to take stock of one's life and plan for the next year. Leave out the holiday aspect and you still have a great story."

She grabbed the paint-can opener that I'd snagged from the counter at the hardware store and began to pop the lid open. I studied her for a moment before I finally pushed aside my concerns and looked for a brush to join her.

She had a point. Just because *A Christmas Carol* took place in December, that didn't mean it *had* to take place during Christmastime. A grumpy man coming face-to-face with how he'd treated everyone in his life and how that put him on the path toward a bleak future was a story we all could understand, with or without the holiday.

Hating the silence that had fallen between us, I moved to speak. "Did you do a lot of plays when you were a kid?"

Clara had started painting a cityscape, so I moved to join her, dipping my brush into the black paint. She glanced over at me and then returned her focus to the backdrop.

"I was Ralph in *A Christmas Story,* Cindy Lou Who—two years in a row—and I was Rudolph in *Santa Stole Christmas,* an original play written by my grandmother." She paused, her expression turning nostalgic as she stared at the ground.

Watching her memories flood to the surface only reminded me of my own memories from yesterday. I understood the reverence you feel when you recall things you'd forgot.

For so long, I'd buried my memories because they hurt. They were a reminder of friendships now broken or people now passed. But watching Clara, I longed to remember. She looked sad but at peace. She was someone who cherished her memories, not someone who ran from them.

And suddenly, I wanted to share my own memories with her. Ones from when I was a kid. I wanted her to know more about me in a way I hadn't wanted anyone to since Nicole died.

Clara had been so open with me, it was time for me to repay the favor.

"I want to take you somewhere," I blurted out before I had actually thought out what I was going to say next.

Clara glanced up at me, her eyes wide. "You want to take me somewhere?" she repeated.

I nodded. I'd already opened Pandora's box. There was no going back now. "Yes. Tomorrow night?"

Clara held my gaze as her expression stilled. She slowly nodded. "Okay." Then her smile emerged, and it made my heart sing. "I can't wait."

"Good." I smiled back at her. "I can't wait, either."

TWENTY
CLARA

I'd lost count how many times today I'd cursed myself for deciding to put on a play with a group of five-year-olds with only three days to prepare. It was like herding cats that were both hungry and tired. By the time lunch rolled around, I was sweating like a stuck pig and my hair clung to my face.

The only thing that brought me joy was the text from Silas telling me that he'd be by my house to pick me up at seven. I couldn't stop the smile that emerged. Silas had actually been a huge help last night. Not only did he stay late to help me paint the backdrop, but he even helped me set everything up so we'd have something to practice in front of today.

He'd cleaned up the paint, carried it back to my room, and lingered in the doorway while I gathered my things. Then he'd walked me to my car.

Something had changed in our relationship. And after last night, I was beginning to believe that I wasn't the only one who felt it. Why else would Silas want to take me somewhere tonight? Why else would he cryptically smile when I asked him for more information? Why else would he say my infamous line, "you'll just have to wait and see"?

Silas had been standoffish since he first knocked on my door, so there was only one way to interpret his sudden invitation—something had changed for him, too.

And I couldn't wait to find out if I was right.

When I got home, I jumped in the shower to wash the day off. I blared Christmas music as I dried my hair and did my makeup. I didn't want to look like I was trying too hard, but I also wanted to look my best.

I wanted him to appreciate what he saw. And when the image of him raking his gaze over my body entered my mind, butterflies began to dive-bomb my stomach.

I picked a baby-blue sweater with a subtle white Christmas pattern across the front and paired it with my dark jeans. I wanted Silas to feel respected when he picked me up. Though I did put on a pair of Christmas ornament earrings—because I wasn't an animal and this was still December.

I was slipping on my tan boots when there was a knock on my door. I hurriedly slid my heel into the boot and pulled up the zipper before I made my way over. Silas was standing on my porch, wearing a black jacket, his cheeks pink from the cold, and an armful of Christmas decorations in his arms.

Never in my life had I been picked up for...whatever this was...and been given a more fitting gift. It was like a bouquet of flowers for the Christmas crazed.

"For me?" I asked. But on further inspection, I started recognizing the items. "What...?"

"You can stop sneaking them over to my house," he said as I stepped out of the way so he could come inside.

His words confused me. "I can what?"

He set the decorations down on the couch and then turned to face me. "You're the one who keeps leaving these all over my yard and porch, right?"

I shook my head. "That does sound like something I would do, but I promise you, I didn't do anything of the sort."

Silas frowned as he stared down at the decorations and then shifted his gaze to his house through my front window. Down to the pile...over to his house. Then he smiled.

"Dog," he whispered.

"Dog?" I asked, wondering how that was the answer to this riddle.

He scrubbed his face with his hand. "Yeah." He paused. "Dog—who you renamed Blitzen—is a service school dropout."

I raised my eyebrows. "He's a what?"

"A service school dropout. I got him back when

Isabelle..." His voice drifted off as his skin paled. I wondered what he was trying not to say. Was it wrong that I wanted to know what seemed to be plaguing him?

I wanted him to keep going. I wanted him to open up to me. But I also didn't want to push him past where he was comfortable. I hoped that, at some point, he would open up to me. And when he did, knowing about his past would be an honor.

Silas cleared his throat. "Anyway, I got Dog for Isabelle. She grew attached to him, so even though he flunked out, I had to take him home." He smiled. "Problem is, you can't really unteach certain things. He must have seen this stuff and fetched them for us."

I couldn't help the smile that emerged. "That is so cute," I said.

Silas's expression softened as he glanced up at me and then back down to the ornament pile. "Yeah. He's a good dog."

Silence fell between us. I stood there, watching Silas, waiting for him to speak first. This was his memory, and I didn't want to interrupt it. Finally, he sighed and glanced over at me. His gaze trailed down my body before he brought it back up.

"You look nice," he said in a way that made my cheeks flush. His smile made my heart pound as he asked, "You ready?"

I wasn't crazy, right? He had to be feeling something too. At least, I hoped he was. It had been too long since a man had paid attention to me. Maybe I was misreading everything. Maybe I was so tired of being alone, that after the tiniest bit of attention from a man I jumped in feetfirst.

Was that what I was doing? Reading into things that weren't there?

On paper, Silas and I didn't make sense. We were exact opposites. I was spontaneous and weird, while he was serious and reserved. I was a fool to think that any kind of relationship could happen between us. I wasn't sure I could make him happy, and if he was still hell-bent on canceling Christmas, I was certain he couldn't make me happy.

So, why did I feel so happy?

Realizing that he was waiting for me to speak, I glanced up and smiled. Whatever that freak-out had been, I was going to keep it buried deep down inside my chest. I wasn't going to let it surface tonight.

My feelings were just that, mine. Silas was just starting to open up to me, and the last thing I wanted to do was make him slam the lid closed on our friendship for good. Silas and I weren't some cosmic couple finally finding each other. We were just two stubborn people life had thrown together.

I was determined to change his mind about the best time of the year, while he was determined to keep the status quo. That was all.

"I'm ready," I said as I reached forward to grasp the door handle.

Silas nodded and just as he turned to follow me out the door, he paused, his gaze falling on Isabelle's tree.

He knit his eyebrows together. "You decorated it," he said.

"Yeah." I pointed at him. "I used the popcorn chain we made."

He studied it before he slowly began to nod. "It looks nice." Then his gaze drifted over to the opposite wall, where I'd stacked up the decorations I'd removed from around the tree. "What's going on here?"

I waved my hand as I reached out to grab his arm. "That's nothing. We should really get going." My fingers wrapped around his forearm and I pulled slightly. I didn't need to go the rounds with him like I had with Abbie. I didn't need people to start thinking that something was wrong with me when I was perfectly fine. In fact, I'd never felt better.

I could already see Silas latching onto Abbie's idea of creating a holiday rehab center here in Grinchland, and that would have the exact opposite result of what I was trying to accomplish during our seven-day deal.

I didn't want Silas to think that Grinchland was having a positive effect on me.

Silas glanced down at my hand and then back up to me. I could see he wanted to press me about it, but I just motioned toward the front door with my head, hoping that would get him to move.

Thankfully, he didn't push me further. Instead, he just

glanced over at the wall and then back to me and then back to the wall. Finally, he turned and followed me out the door.

We were quiet as we walked out to his car that was still running in my driveway. I went to open the door, but he beat me to it, his fingers brushing mine in the process. Jolts of electricity rushed up my arm from the sensation of his skin against mine.

He cleared his throat as he held open the door, and I slipped onto the passenger seat. He did a once-over as if to make sure I was fully inside before he gently shut the door. Once he got in the car, he asked me if the temperature was okay and pulled out of my driveway.

I nodded before I peeked over at him, appreciating his profile. Silas was a handsome man. Even more so now that he wasn't constantly glowering at me. He must have felt me staring because he glanced over at me before he frowned.

"What?" he asked.

I shrugged as I moved my attention out the window. "Nothing," I said.

He paused. "Okay."

"It's just that you're much better looking when you're not glaring at everyone." The words tumbled from my lips before I could stop them. My cheeks heated as I peeked over at him, wondering if I'd said too much.

"You think I'm good-looking?"

I cleared my throat and shifted in my seat. "I do

believe that my exact words were *better looking*. Not good-looking."

He glanced over at me and then back to the road. His left wrist was resting on the steering wheel, and his right arm was propped up on the console between us. His body was slightly tipped toward me. He seemed relaxed and unbothered by what I said.

"I heard *good-looking*," he said before turning toward me and flashing me a smile.

I rolled my eyes. "We hear what we want to."

I watched as his expression softened as if a painful memory had suddenly washed over him. He swallowed hard, his Adam's apple bobbing up and down before his jaw muscles flinched.

"It's been hard to be happy since Nicole..." His voice drifted off.

I wanted him to keep going. I wanted to know more about him. I was beginning to care about this man. I wanted to help even if there wasn't much I could do other than listen.

"Was Nicole your wife?" I asked, my voice hushed with reverence for her memory.

He glanced over at me before he slowly began to nod. "She passed away three years ago." He swallowed. "On Christmas Eve."

My heart sank and my entire body went numb. No wonder this man hated the holiday. It was a reminder of everything he'd lost.

"I'm so sorry," I whispered, worried that I'd pushed him to talk about her when he wasn't ready.

He chuckled. "Thing is, she loved Christmas, and she would have hated that I got it banned." He grew silent as he was lost in a memory.

I folded my arms across my chest, hoping that he felt my support. I was willing to listen, but I was equally ready to let it all go.

He finally glanced over at me as if he'd suddenly remembered that I was sitting next to him. He held my gaze for a moment before he turned his attention back to the road and merged onto the freeway.

"Nicole would have loved you," he said as he flipped on his blinker and moved over a lane.

"I would love to have met her. If Isabelle is any indication of how great she was, I bet she was pretty amazing."

Silas nodded. "She was the best."

Silence fell between us as Silas drove. I settled back in my seat and allowed us to just be. There was no need for talking. There was no need for explaining. We had both lost someone important to us. It was a pain that many didn't understand.

And there was nothing more that needed to be said.

I was surprised when I saw the sign for Georgetown. I allowed myself to hope that he was taking me here for the one reason I'd come here in December. And when he pulled into the parking lot of Mistletoe Meadow, *the* Christmas lights display in Maine, I cheered. But when I realized my reaction might deter him, I slapped my hand over my mouth and turned to him, my eyes wide.

Silas just chuckled and shook his head. "I figured you'd react this way," he said as he waited for a yellow VW bug to pull out of a parking spot before he promptly took it.

Just as he turned off the engine, I stuck my arm out, stopping him. "Wait. Are you telling me that you're *voluntarily* taking me here?" My eyes were wide as I stared at him.

Silas shifted in his seat so he could face me. "I'm voluntarily taking you here," he repeated.

I frowned. "What? Why?"

He glanced at me and then out the window toward the Christmas lights twinkling above. "You shared your traditions with me. I figured I'd share one with you."

My eyes bugged from my head. "*You* have Christmas traditions?" I narrowed my eyes. "Are you a closeted Christmas fan?"

His lips were flat as he studied me. "I don't have Christmas traditions, but I grew up in a family that did."

I glanced toward Mistletoe Meadows. "This was one of them?"

Silas pulled on the door release and started to climb out of his truck. "This is one of them."

Pure joy raced through me as I scrambled to open the door. Nothing could have prepared me for how it would feel to have the Grinch of Grinchland tell me that he wanted to share a Christmas memory with me. It was like I'd been given the biggest gift of all time, and there was no way I was going to waste a second of it.

I was going to soak up this moment for as long as I could because I knew that Silas had a limit. I didn't know when his patience for doing something that was this steeped in Christmas would expire.

I was surprised when we got to the entrance booth and Silas pulled out his wallet to pay. I didn't say anything as he took the tickets and walked me through the front gate. I kept quiet as he started to guide me around to the displays and told me about them.

I felt like I was in some sort of Christmas twilight zone. My eyes felt dry because I refused to blink, fearing that if I did, this would all go away. This moment was so strange, and yet it was also so right. There was no way I was going to miss it.

I knew Christmas was powerful, I just didn't realize it was this powerful.

I almost fainted when Silas stopped at the hot chocolate vendor and offered to buy me a cup. I decided to press my luck and ask him if he was going to get one too, fully expecting him to shut me down, but to my surprise, he shrugged and said yes.

With our cups of cocoa in hand, we proceeded to the next display.

"Isabelle would love this one," I whispered as I stared at the lights that had been twisted into the image of an ice-skating couple. He was behind her and they both had their hands outstretched like they were moving in sync with one another.

"She would love this," Silas whispered from behind me.

Shivers raced down my spine as I tipped my head ever so slightly to the side so I could see where he was. He was no more than an inch behind me. Even though he wasn't touching me, I could feel him standing there. The warmth of his body emanating to mine.

I wanted to read into his position. I wanted to think that he wanted to be close to me, that he just might care for me like I was beginning to care for him.

Was that possible?

"You should bring her here sometime," I said before I really thought about what those words meant.

When he didn't respond, guilt coated my chest. Why had I spoken? Why did I have to ruin this magical moment? I just wanted Isabelle to be happy. That girl wanted Christmas so bad, and I couldn't understand why her father was so resistant to let her experience it.

"It's not that I don't want to." His words were soft and broken.

I turned to face him. His gaze was downturned and his shoulders were slumped. I wasn't sure if I should speak, so I just settled in so he could talk.

"I'm scared I will lose my daughter just like I lost my

wife." He shifted the hot cocoa cup from hand to hand. "That can't happen. I will break."

I studied him. I couldn't understand what it was about Christmas that had such a chokehold on him, but I wanted to help. I wanted to fix what had happened. I wanted to show him that it was just a holiday. It didn't have the power that he seemed so convinced it had.

I didn't think before I acted. I reached out and grabbed his hand. He froze, his gaze drifting over to study our hands. Suddenly, he turned his palm and opened his fingers so I could slip mine in. Then he paused, our bodies next to each other. Supporting each other.

He didn't let go as we moved to the next display. He held my hand the entire walk to the gazebo at the end of the trail. The wooden structure was covered in fairy lights and all sorts of Christmas foliage. Just as we went up the steps, Silas paused.

I was one step above him, which made me just an inch shorter than him. I turned to see what I had missed. Silas was staring above my head, so I followed his gaze.

"Is that...mistletoe?" he asked, bringing his gaze level with mine.

My cheeks warmed as I studied him before I glanced back up at the very obvious mistletoe above us. "I'm not sure," I said, my tone teasing.

He took a step up so he was towering above me. Slowly, he reached up to cradle my cheek before he slid his fingers through my hair and firmly placed his hand behind my head. "I've heard that a mistletoe kiss is unlike anything you've ever experienced," he whispered as he brought his lips inches away from mine.

"Oh really," I said softly as I glanced down to his lips and then back up to meet his gaze.

"Really," he said, his half smile emerging, which caused butterflies to dive-bomb my stomach. "I've never experienced one, but I'm always up to try something new."

"It's good to have an open mind."

He nodded. "I'm learning to be better."

My hands found his arms before they slid up so I could rest my arms on his shoulders. "You're doing such a good job."

His lips captured mine, and all further words flew from my mind. All that existed in the moment was Silas and I. His lips against mine. His hands on my body. Our breaths intertwining.

My lips were swollen and my eyes felt hazy when he pulled back. His gaze was full of desire as he studied me.

"Dear God, woman," he murmured as he rested his forehead against mine. "That was incredible." He pulled back slightly so he could cup my cheek once more. Then he gently ran his thumb over my bottom lip.

I nodded. "Agreed."

He studied me before he stared at my lips. I wasn't sure what he was going to do, but when his lips crashed into mine again, I decided that I was done with thinking for the night.

TWENTY-ONE
SILAS

I woke up thinking about Clara. In all honesty, she hadn't left my mind ever since I dropped her off at her house. After I kissed her, pressed up against her front door until she was panting. After I let my hands roam over her body, memorizing her curves. After her hands clutched my jacket like she never wanted to let me go.

It felt good, kissing her.

It felt right.

I both loved and loathed how right it felt to be close to her. To touch her. To want her. And for her to want me back? It was perfection. So much so that I found myself humming while I shaved, doing a little dance in my closet while I got dressed, and barging into Isabelle's room like an announcer for a TV show.

Isabelle loved it. She could feel my energy and matched it. She skipped around her room while I helped her pick out an outfit, sang at the top of her lungs while I packed her lunch, and demanded that I twirl her as we walked out to the car to get to school.

I laughed—something I hadn't done in a long time. But it felt right. After all, I was doing a lot of things that I hadn't done in a long time.

When Clara emerged from her house, I paused to take her in. I wanted her to know how I felt about our date last night. A shy smile emerged as she studied me. There was a secret between us, and I loved that we were the only two people in the entire world who knew what had happened.

Her cheeks flushed and she focused on her car before she glanced back up at me. I waved and called out, "Good morning."

She only nodded as she unlocked her driver's door and then slipped onto her seat. I wanted to walk over to her and demand that she acknowledge me, but I suspected that her hesitancy had more to do with Isabelle being present than with her suddenly finding me repulsive and never wanting to speak to me again.

At least one of us had self-control.

I tried to keep my composure as I dropped Isabelle off outside of her classroom. I wanted to see Clara again, and I was disappointed that she hadn't been in the hallway to greet me. I angled my body in the doorway in an effort to catch a glimpse of her.

With my weight on one leg as I attempted to peer deeper into the classroom, I heard someone clear their throat from behind me. Heat flushed my body as I turned to see Maria standing there with her eyebrows raised. My gaze flicked over to Clara, who was standing next to her, clutching a stack of papers to her chest. She had an amused smile on her lips.

Shit. I'd been caught red-handed.

"Did you need something, Mayor?" Maria asked.

I straightened and adjusted my suit coat. "Nope." I paused, desperate for a reasonable explanation as to why I was trying so hard to see into the classroom, but nothing rational was coming to mind. So, I went with the next best thing: the truth.

"I was looking for Ms. Snow." I gave a pointed look to Clara, and when her cheeks flushed, I took satisfaction from being able to get her to react that way.

"Oh?" Maria glanced over at Clara. "And what do you need to talk to her about?"

I cleared my throat as I shoved my hands into the front pocket of my pants and tipped slightly toward Maria. "What *did* I need to talk to her about?"

The only thing that was flowing through my mind was our kiss last night and how badly I wanted to reenact it, but I doubted that Maria would want to hear about that. And I doubted Clara wanted me talking to her boss about it.

"Probably about the play," Clara said as she glanced over to me with her eyes wide as if prompting me to play along.

"The play," I said, probably a tad too loud from the way Maria's eyebrows went up even farther. "I need to talk to her about the play," I said, bringing my voice down a bit too low. I winced. Why couldn't I just act normal?

Maria glanced from me over to Clara and then back to me. "Well, here she is," Maria said as she glanced back at Clara once more before she shook her head and continued walking down the hallway.

Now that we were alone, I glanced over at Clara, my gaze instantly dropping to her lips before I forced it back up. "I'm sorry about that," I whispered.

Clara was studying me with her lips tipped up in a shy smile. She shook her head. "It's okay."

I leaned in. "I was dropping off Isabelle."

She nodded. "I figured."

I glanced down at the ground. "And...I was trying to see you." I flicked my gaze up to meet hers.

"I figured," she whispered, her voice turning breathless.

My heart pounded from the sound. Thoughts of our kisses and the soft way she moaned against my lips raced through my mind, and it was taking all my strength not to press her against the lockers and kiss her once more.

"So can I see you tonight?"

She nodded. "You can." Then she leaned in. "We have practice," she whispered.

That was not what I meant. I preferred my one-on-one time with Clara.

"But afterward..." She took a step closer to me and peered up at me through her long, dark lashes. "If you want, you can come over."

I didn't try to hide my smile. Instead, I just stared down at her, enjoying the flirty way she met my gaze as if she were challenging me.

"I can?"

She nodded.

"Do you have another Christmas activity that you want to show me?"

She shrugged. "You'll just have to wait and see." She tucked her hair behind her ear before she started to walk toward the doorway to her classroom.

"Is this a required activity?" I asked.

She paused before she flicked her gaze over her shoulder. "No." And with that, she disappeared into the classroom, leaving me alone in the hallway.

My heart was racing as I walked out to my car. Her words echoed in my mind like the cave walls of the Grinch's lair. This wasn't required. Did that mean she wanted to spend time with me? Was this...a date?

Did I want it to be a date?

In all honesty, yesterday had felt like a date to me even though I'd packaged it up in my mind as just another one of the Christmas activities she was forcing me to participate in. But today felt different. Today felt wanted.

Desired.

That thought plagued me all day. I tried to keep my

head straight as I listened to Todd during our morning meeting. I tried to keep my focus during my meeting with sanitation. I tried to keep Clara out of my mind as I answered emails and cleaned out my desk, but I failed miserably.

She had wiggled her way into my life and was becoming impossible to forget.

That night, during play practice, I tried to keep my gaze down and my attention on helping the kids find their marks and understand their cues, but I kept getting distracted by the way Clara's nose wrinkled when she thought something was cute, or the way her smile grew big every time Isabelle practically yelled her lines.

Apparently to Clara, Scrooge was the best part for Isabelle. And even though Isabelle had no idea who Scrooge was, she was determined to give the part her all. That little girl was acting her heart out, and Clara was eating it up.

And I was falling even harder for Clara as I watched her encourage, smile at, and cheer on Isabelle every time she delivered her lines without messing up.

I never thought I would feel so much desire for a woman who wasn't paying attention to me. Back when I was dating Nicole, I loved it when she smiled at me from the other side of the room. When she would sneak up next to me and grab my hand. Or when her gaze held mine as she walked toward me.

But watching a woman love my daughter—that was a

level of attraction that I had never experienced before. It sent a whole new level of desire coursing through me.

So when play practice was over and I'd fed, bathed, and pajamaed my daughter, I waited for Isabelle to fall asleep in her bed before I scooped her up and made my way over to Clara's.

After Isabelle was tucked in under Clara's covers and we'd made our way out into the hallway, I didn't waste any time pinning Clara against the wall and kissing her with all my pent-up feelings. She giggled against my lips as her hands found my chest and her fingers curled into the fabric of my shirt like she'd been waiting for this moment. I growled and wrapped my arms around her waist and hoisted her up so she was higher than me.

She parted her lips and my tongue danced around hers. Our lips moved in unison as if we both wanted to feel and touch as much as we could. She wrapped her legs around my waist, her blonde hair falling around my head, creating a curtain around us.

I didn't break off our kiss as I carried her from the hall to the living room. Once I felt the couch bump the back of my legs, I lowered myself down. Clara straddled me, her arms on either side of my head and her hands holding onto the back of the couch.

I let my hands explore her waist, her hips, until I brought them to her thighs and dug my fingertips into the soft material of her jeans in an effort to bring her closer to me. She complied, rising up slightly onto her knees so she could press her chest against mine. She never broke our kiss, instead, her lips drew my face upward.

I could have kissed Clara all night, but she seemed to have a different plan as, suddenly, she pulled back.

"I have something for you," she said. She pressed her fingertips to her lips a few times as she moved to sit further back on my thighs.

I wanted to yank her back to me and kiss her again, but she looked so excited, so I just knit my eyebrows together. "You do?" I asked as I glanced around, wondering what on earth she could have gotten me.

She nodded and started to shift her weight, so I helped her off my lap. I settled back against the couch and watched as she hurriedly left the living room. Now alone, I blew out my breath and tipped my head back against the wall. I closed my eyes and just allowed myself to feel. To be in this moment.

Kissing Clara was quickly becoming my drug, and that both scared and exhilarated me.

"I found it," she sang out.

I glanced up to see her enter the room from the kitchen. She had a white bag in her hand and a mischievous grin on her lips.

I frowned. "What is that?"

She crossed the space between us and sat down on the couch, her knees pressed into my thigh. "Open it," she said as she dropped the bag in my lap.

I studied her before I slowly took the bag. "You should

know that I hate surprises," I said as I found one of the handles and then the second one.

"I know, but this is a good surprise," she said, her voice steeped in excitement.

I narrowed my eyes but then decided to stop being so cynical and just open her gift. As soon as I saw the green and red fabric of a Christmas sweater, I whipped my gaze over to meet hers. She was grinning from ear to ear with her hands clasped in front of her like she was trying with all her might to contain her excitement.

"It's a—"

"It's a Christmas sweater!" she squealed as she moved to shake out the sleeves of the sweater that I was now holding up in front of me.

"—sweater." I finally finished.

"Do you like it?"

No. I hated it. But loved how excited it made her, so I forced a smile. "It's interesting."

She sighed as she studied me. "You can't wear—"

"Basic?"

She paused before she nodded. "That's right, you can't wear *basic* clothes all the time." Then she glanced around the room. "You don't have to worry about anyone seeing you in here. It's just me," she said as she brought her gaze back to meet mine.

I glanced from the sweater over to Clara and then back to the sweater. "You really want me to wear this?" I asked. Every part of my being was telling me not to, but all I wanted to do was make Clara happy, even if it meant putting this offending item on my body.

She smiled and nodded. "Yes," she whispered.

I shifted my weight until I was sitting in the middle of the couch cushion. I grabbed the back of my collar and pulled it off in one swift motion. I heard Clara inhale, and I glanced over to see that her cheeks had reddened and her gaze was trained on my chest.

Satisfaction rose up inside of me as I smirked at her. If I was going to wear this ridiculous sweater, at least I was going to have some fun doing it. But when her gaze met mine and I saw the heat and desire that she had for me, suddenly, this was no longer a game.

This was something so much more.

I pulled the sweater on, and Clara climbed back onto my lap and kissed me until I felt like I couldn't breathe. Even though wearing this sweater went against everything I'd stood for the last three years, I suddenly didn't care. All I wanted in this moment was Clara.

For the first time in a long time, I felt alive.

For the first time in a long time, I felt...free.

TWENTY-TWO
CLARA

Things had completely changed between Silas and me. He was the last thing I thought about when I went to bed and the first thing I thought about when I woke up. I spent the morning wondering what he was doing and even tried to catch a glimpse of him from my house as I dressed and made myself breakfast.

My entire body warmed when I saw him walk by his kitchen window, and I feared if I didn't hurry, I was going to miss seeing him even though it had only been six hours since he'd left my house. He'd stayed over last night until the wee hours of the morning. We made out on the couch and then snuggled under a blanket while we watched *Die Hard*—his favorite Christmas movie.

I wanted to object—*Die Hard* was not a Christmas movie—but he seemed so excited to share it with me. Plus, he'd been such a good sport about doing all of my Christmas traditions, that I decided to give him this one.

After the movie was over, I straightened on the couch and declared that I had been right, *Die Hard* was indeed *not* a Christmas movie. I met his gaze head-on in anticipation of his argument.

Instead of fighting, Silas just grabbed my arms and yanked me to his chest, where he kissed me with such passion and fury that my objection flew from my mind and all that existed was him and I.

We were all that mattered.

And when his gaze caught mine as we both climbed into our cars, and I saw the intensity with which he was staring at me, I knew he felt the same. That thought both thrilled and terrified me.

By all accounts, Silas and I were opposites. We were two sides of a coin that didn't make sense. He was grumpy, and I was Christmas. He was black and white, and I was glitter and everything festive. He shouldn't want me, and I shouldn't want him. But for some reason, none of that mattered. He was the person that got my heart racing. And from the way he kissed me last night, I did the same for him.

Thankfully, twenty-four five-year-olds all breaking down because they forgot their lines provided the distraction I needed from my thoughts of Silas. We spent most of the day rehearsing the play until I called it good—or good enough—and declared we were doing arts and crafts until the end of the day.

I didn't bother to go home. Tonight was opening night, and I needed to get some last-minute things ready. As the time grew closer to six, I began to feel on edge. Every time someone appeared in the doorway of the gym, my gaze whipped over to see if it was Silas and Isabelle. But each time I saw another child's parents enter, my stomach fell.

I had confidence that he was going to show up, but there was a part of me, a teeny, tiny part of me that feared this was all too much. That he was going to wake up and realize I'd pushed Christmas on the Christmas-hating mayor, and he was going to revolt.

"Ms. Snow!" Isaac's mom exclaimed as she approached me.

I blinked a few times, forcing my thoughts from Silas. "Hey, Mrs. Parkes." I stepped closer to her. "Everything okay?"

Her grin grew wider. "I don't know how you did it, but I just wanted to say thank you for bringing a bit of Christmas back to this town. I thought Silas would come to his senses eventually, but as the years went on, that hope slowly died." She sighed. "But then you showed up and *bang*"—she clapped her hands—"Christmas."

I glanced around, fearing that Silas would overhear and realize that I'd successfully wiggled the holiday that he hated back into Grinchland. That may have been the reason I initially did all of this, but things had changed. They'd changed a lot.

"I'm glad you're happy."

"Maybe next year, we'll actually be able to call it *A Christmas Carol*, instead of just *A Carol*." She tapped the tip of her nose before she pointed her finger at me.

I nodded. "Maybe."

She sighed. "Well, just thought I'd say thank you. Isaac is so excited to be *Christmas*"—she mouthed the word—"past."

"I'm glad."

Mrs. Turnbow walked past just as those words left my lips. Realizing that I hadn't fulfilled my side of the Pudgie the penguin bargain, I gave Mrs. Parkes an apologetic smile and then hurried after Catalina's mom.

"Mrs. Turnbow?" I asked as I reached out and brushed my fingers against her elbow in an effort to get her attention.

Mrs. Turnbow stopped and turned. "Ms. Snow?" she asked.

Just then, from the corner of my eyes, I saw Silas walk into the gym. I hated that seeing him caused my gaze to go fuzzy and my heart to pick up speed. All I wanted to do was look at him, but I couldn't. Not when Mrs. Turnbow was staring at me expectantly.

So I pulled my gaze from Silas and focused my attention. "I heard that you have excluded Isabelle St. Nick from Catalina's party." I folded my arms across my chest. "It is school policy that if you are inviting other members of the class that you invite *all* of her classmates." Heat pricked the back of my neck as a protective surge rose up inside of me.

No one messes with my—

I stopped that thought, and my eyes widened as I realized the word that was going to complete that sentence: daughter. I almost called Isabelle my daughter.

What was wrong with me?

Mrs. Turnbow's eyes were wide when I brought my attention back to her. Minus that brain aneurism, I still needed to focus on the task at hand.

"Well, Ms. Snow, I would have invited Isabelle to Catalina's *Christmas* party in Jordan, but since her father is the man who explicitly banned Christmas in our town, I thought that would be in bad taste."

My surprised expression must have been exactly what she was expecting because her eyebrow went up in anticipation of my response. All I could manage was a weak, "Oh," before all of my words left me.

"Oh is right. So next time, maybe don't assume that I'm purposely leaving a child out." She turned on her heel and headed toward the chairs the janitor had set up earlier in the day.

I wanted to walk after her. I wanted to apologize for assuming the worst. It hadn't even crossed my mind that Isabelle hadn't been invited to the party because of the type of party it was.

My gaze drifted over to Silas, who was watching me. He smiled and gave me a thumbs-up. I didn't know what I was going to say to him, so all I could do was offer him a weak thumbs-up in return.

Silas loved Isabelle more than anything else in his life. He would do anything for her. But what was he going to do when faced with either continuing his ban on Christmas or making it so his daughter got invited to parties?

He couldn't very well tell Mrs. Turnbow to change the theme of the party so his daughter could go. His powers didn't reach that far.

This was a conundrum. I wasn't sure he knew what he would do, and I wasn't sure I wanted to be the person to present it to him. Things with Silas were going well because he knew I wasn't going to push him when it came to Isabelle. But if she was feeling left out, maybe it was time for Silas to reconsider his ban.

Luckily, I was too busy getting the kids organized to come face-to-face with Silas. The kids were back behind the plywood cutouts that Todd had made and Silas and I had painted. They were nervous but looked adorable. Mrs. Kellington, the high school home economics teacher, had offered to sew costumes last minute.

Once word got out that I was going against the ban and hosting this play, everyone in town came out of the woodwork to help. It gave me hope that if, someday, Silas saw the error in his ways, perhaps Christmas could return to Grinchland.

One could hope.

I stayed in the back to direct the children out. We waited in anticipation while the parents and family members took their seats. Once the clock hit seven, I stepped out and did a short introduction. I thanked the people who helped put the play together and the kids for being such good sports. Everyone cheered, and I could feel Silas's gaze on me.

It warmed me in every way possible. I wanted him to always look at me this way, and I feared how it would change when I confronted him about Isabelle. Would he hate me?

I pushed those thoughts from my mind as I returned to the kids. Right now, it was about their hard work and this play. The opening scene was set up by the sixth-grade volunteers, so I knelt down in front of Isabelle and met her gaze head-on.

"You ready, girlfriend?" I asked.

Isabelle nodded. She had a white beard hooked around her ears and a suit that was about two sizes too big, but she looked excited.

I knew it probably wasn't kosher, but I pulled her into a quick hug. I'd fallen in love with this little girl and I wanted the best for her. I was going to try my hardest to get her everything a little girl deserved.

"Break a leg," I whispered before I turned her toward the entrance.

It took her a moment before she started to timidly walk out onto the makeshift stage we'd set up. The spotlight—which was just a flashlight controlled by the janitor, Mr. Rex—turned on her. She stood there, frozen in place.

I waited...and waited...for her to speak. In all the rehearsals, she had been our shining star, so her lack of confidence now was out of character.

I watched as her skin paled, and a weak, "Daddy," could be heard throughout the silent gym.

I'd never seen someone move as fast as Silas did in that moment. He was out of his chair and to her side in the blink of an eye. It took a moment for me to process what was happening as he scooped her up and cradled her in his arms.

Then he turned and faced the audience. "This play is over. Everyone go home. The ban is still in effect." His voice boomed through the air.

Finally, my brain caught up with what was going on and my feet started moving in Silas's direction. He didn't waste any time as he gathered Isabelle's things and headed toward the doors that led outside.

"Silas," I called after him, but he didn't stop.

He kept moving, and I had to run to catch up with him. He finally cut me a break when he had to stop to put Isabelle in the car and load her things in the bed of his truck. He'd slammed her door and was headed to the driver's side when I reached out and grabbed his arm. He froze.

"Silas," I said, my voice breathy from the impromptu jog I'd just done to reach him. "Can we talk?" I dipped down with the hopes of catching his gaze. I needed him to take a moment and breathe instead of just reacting.

"This is over," he whispered.

I blinked as I knit my eyebrows together. "What?"

Finally, he glanced up at me with a look of fire in his eyes. His jaw was set and his body was tense. "This"—he motioned between us—"is over. Christmas in Grinchland is banned. It has been banned for the last three years and will continue to be banned for as long as I can keep it that way."

"But, Silas—"

"Stop trying to change things. You don't live here. You're only here for three months and then you're leaving." His eyes narrowed. "I was being reckless."

"Reckless?" I stared at him. Was he serious? Why was he doing this? "Isabelle just had some stage fright, that's all. That happens sometimes. If you had just waited—"

"No. No, you don't understand." He shook his head as he turned to grab his door handle.

I reached out and grabbed his hand. This wasn't what I wanted. I wanted to help, not drive him away. "Isabelle wasn't invited to Catalina's party because it's a Christmas party, Silas. A *Christmas* party."

Silas paused as I watched my words sink in. For a

moment, I allowed myself to believe that he was going to change his mind, and the longer he stayed quiet, the more hopeful I became. Until he resolutely nodded his head and yanked open the door handle. "Then Janice was right to exclude Isabelle."

"But, Silas—"

"Goodbye, Clara."

Tears began to form on my eyelids as I helplessly watched Silas climb into his truck and slam his door. I moved to the patch of grass in front of his hood as he started his engine and his lights turned on. He put his truck into reverse and looked up, his gaze landing on me for a moment before he brought his arm up to the passenger seat and twisted so he could see over his shoulder.

He didn't look at me again as he straightened out his truck, put it into drive, and took off out of the parking lot.

I waited for a few minutes with the hopes that Silas would come to his senses and drive back.

I waited in vain.

TWENTY-THREE
CLARA

I'd been stupid to think that all Silas needed was a good night's sleep and a big hearty breakfast to come to his senses. I spent all morning on edge because I expected him to knock on my door with some grand gesture and apologize for being a cotton-headed, ninny muggins last night.

I really needed to stop waiting for Silas to do things.

His house was eerily quiet when I walked out to my car to head to school. Just as I pulled out of my driveway, I looked over to see that Pudgie was gone. There wasn't a spec of Christmas to be seen at his house.

I sighed as I idled at the end of my driveway. I wanted to march up to his front door, pound on it, and demand that he put it back. After all, we still had eight hours left in our deal and he'd just broken it by taking Pudgie down... but I didn't have the drive to fight Silas anymore.

I was trying to ignore it, but my heart had been

broken. I'd allowed myself to fall for Silas, and instead of returning my affection, he decided to pull out my heart and stomp on it before throwing it into the blender and pulverizing it.

Silas had made his feelings pretty clear last night when he drove off and never came back. And now Pudgie? That was the final nail in the coffin of our relationship—or whatever we had.

Isabelle wasn't at school, and most of the kids were down in the dumps that they never got to perform the play. I decided to just spend the day doing kid things. After all, winter break was just around the corner. No learning really took place the last few days anyway.

I was grateful for the weekend when the last bell rang and my kids shuffled out of the classroom. I helped with bus pickup but decided not to linger as I grabbed my jacket and purse and headed out of the building.

As I neared my car, I paused. A man was standing next to it with his head dipped down. For a moment, I allowed myself to hope it was Silas, but as I got closer, I realized it was Todd. I frowned as I dug my keys out of my purse.

"Can I help you with something?" I asked as I located my car key and stepped around Todd to shove it into the lock. "Is there another city ordinance that you have decided to cite me for?" I glanced up at him, hoping that he would pick up on my sarcasm and just leave me alone. I wasn't in the mood to think about Silas.

"I'm here solely as a friend."

I raised my eyebrows. "My friend? Or are you Max?" I didn't have time for Silas's makeshift wingman. If Todd was here to try to get me to forgive that man, I wasn't going to bite.

Todd chuckled before he cleared his throat. My instinct had been right, he'd gotten my reference, so what was his story?

He didn't look like he was going to just give me this information without getting something in return. He studied me for a moment before he said, "Will you come with me for a second? I have something I want to show you at my house."

I stared at him while a war raged inside of me. Part of me wanted to follow him because I was a curious person. Perhaps Todd would finally explain how he knew about the Balsam Hill ornaments. But the other part of me was determined to just keep my head down, finish out my time here in Grinchland, and then never look back.

Grinchland and I were like yellow and snow. Never meant to mix.

But Todd looked earnest, and he had come in clutch when I needed him for the play, so I kind of owed him.

I sighed and nodded. "I'll follow you."

Todd's smile was wide, and I almost felt bad for my initial reaction. I would have apologized, but he was quick to point out his Honda Civic, promising not to lose me before he headed to his car. I pulled open my driver's door and climbed into my car. I pulled out of my parking spot and idled while he did the same.

He waved for me to follow before turning his car to the left and taking off.

Todd was true to his word as we drove the streets of Grinchland. He was mindful of where I was and even pulled off when he got through a red light and I didn't. Eventually, we stopped in front of a small rambler with a large front yard. A front yard that would be perfect for decorating with Balsam Hill ornaments.

I turned my engine off after Todd climbed out of his car and shut his door. He waited for me to join him before he nodded toward his house.

"Come on in."

"Okay," I said hesitantly. "I've seen a lot of murder mystery movies start off this way." I laughed but there was a nervous hint to it.

Todd looked over at me. "I'm not going to murder you," he said, his eyes wide.

"I know," I lied. Truth was, I didn't *really* know. But I had a hunch that Todd wouldn't hurt a fly. "That's why it was a joke."

Todd studied me as he if needed visual confirmation that I trusted him. So I gave him a wide smile.

"You were going to show me something?" I raised my eyebrows in an effort to urge him to continue with why he'd brought me here.

Todd blinked and nodded like he'd suddenly been

snapped out of the confused trance my joke had put him in. "Right," he said as he hurried to the front door and pulled his keys from his pocket.

Soon we were standing in his foyer, and he was waiting for me to finish taking off my boots. When I was done, I straightened and smiled up at him.

"I'm ready," I said.

He extended his hand to a dark oak door to our left. "It's downstairs."

I glanced from the door to Todd and then back to the door. "About the murder—"

"Just open the door," Todd said with an exasperated tone.

"Okay, okay." I reached out and turned the door handle.

I wasn't sure what I thought Todd was going to show me, but an entire basement full of Christmas decorations that would have rivaled Gran's collection in its prime was not on my bingo card. I didn't know where to look first, and I felt like I was a kid in a candy store, just standing there, gaping.

"You're..." I was struggling to catch my breath. "You're a..." I turned to stare at Todd, whose smile mimicked that of a dad on the day of his child's birth. "You're a closet Christmas-er."

He frowned, drawing his eyebrows together as if he were thinking about what I'd just said. "I, um, I wouldn't call myself that."

"Oh my gosh! You have the Hallmark Santa of 1995?" I asked as I sidestepped a life-sized Rudolph to pick up the coveted glass Santa that took Gran three years to finally get her hands on.

"Yep. Found it in a flea market in Jersey a few years ago."

I reverently turned it around in my hands a few times. "Oh! Where did you find the complete Tinson Hall reindeer set?" I set the Santa down so I could give my full attention to the tiny tin reindeers in front of me. Gran passed before she ever got her hands on even one.

"That was a gift from my aunt."

I glanced up at him. "It's beautiful." Thoughts of my own pieces back in Winter Springs made my heart ache. So many memories were wrapped up in those items. I missed them. I missed Gran.

I sighed as I glanced around. It was such a shame that Todd was forced to hide all of these things. "Too bad you live in Grinchland. These pieces deserve to be showcased."

Todd studied me before he shrugged. "You don't know the full story, do you?"

I paused as I flicked my gaze over to him and then back down. "About Nicole?"

"Nicole and Isabelle."

I paused at the mention of Silas's daughter. I knew bits and pieces, but not the full thing. And it hurt that Silas didn't want to tell me. "I know some things."

Todd reached out and grabbed a porcelain teddy bear and transferred it from one hand to another. "Nicole was the biggest Christmas fiend that I'd ever met. Her decorations rivaled Whoville. She was constantly dragging Silas all over the place in search of the next hot item. On Christmas Eve three years ago, there was an accident. Silas and Isabelle were in the car." Todd paused. "Nicole passed away."

My heart broke for that little family.

"But it wasn't just that. Isabelle went from a happy, chatty two-year-old to not speaking for months. Silas took her to every psychologist he could to get answers. She finally came around, but the consensus was to keep anything that had to do with that night away from her."

"That's why he banned Christmas."

Todd nodded. "How could we say no to a grieving husband and a terrified father? If it protected Isabelle, we, as a town, would do whatever we could." He paused. "And maybe we thought, after a few years, he'd realize that she was safe and bring it back." His gaze met mine again. "When you showed up, I thought for sure you'd be the person to help him see the sun and get him out from under his dark cloud. It seemed to be working until..."

"The play."

Todd nodded. "The play. Now I fear he will never repeal the ban and we'll be stuck Christmasless forever."

"Do you think Isabelle was slipping back to the silence?"

Todd shrugged. "I don't know. But Silas won't ever take another chance."

I glanced around before blowing out my breath. "What do you want me to do?"

"I don't think there's anything you can do." He glanced around as well. "I guess I just thought you should know the full story. Maybe it would help you understand the history of Grinchland. The history of Silas."

I studied the floor for a moment before I glanced up to meet his gaze. I didn't know what to do with the story he'd told me. Not when I was pretty certain that Silas hated me. Whatever we had was over, even if I wanted things to be different.

"Thanks for sharing this with me." I narrowed my eyes. "I knew I had another Christmas aficionado on my hands." I shook my finger at him. "I was right."

He chuckled. "You were."

I spent the next fifteen minutes picking up rare Christmas decorations and gushing over the fact that he'd located them. His cheeks reddened with pride as he relayed the story of how he acquired each one. By the time I left, I was sad that I was leaving Grinchland. Todd and I had become fast friends.

He made me promise not to tell Silas that he was the one who told me the whole story. I made an "x" across my chest and held up my right hand at a ninety-degree angle. That seemed to appease him, and he waited with his front door open as I climbed into my driver's seat and pulled out of his drive. Once I was heading down his street, he waved and shut the door.

When I got home, I lingered in the driveway with Todd's words rolling around in my mind. My gaze kept slipping over to Silas's house, where the curtains were still drawn. Tears filled my eyes as I thought about the pain that little family had experienced. And how I had been completely insensitive to what he'd gone through.

Suddenly, my lawn decorations didn't bring me as much joy as they used to. Now, they were a representation of my thoughtless behavior. I wanted them gone. I wanted to give Silas a moment of peace. A moment to heal with his daughter.

The last thing I ever wanted to do was hurt that little girl. I loved her so much. And if taking them down meant keeping her safe, I'd do that.

It was the least I could do.

After I put my keys and purse in the house, I made my way out to the front porch and reached down to flip off the power bank. All the lights in my yard went dark.

TWENTY-FOUR
SILAS

One week later

I may have gone to the extreme, but I kept Isabelle inside for a good three days with the drapes drawn just to make sure that there was no sign of her retreating into herself. I lived in fear for the first forty-eight hours that I was going to lose my daughter, but by Monday morning, she was just as bouncy and active as ever.

I wanted to keep her home from school until the new year, but she wasn't having it. When she came down dressed in a tutu and a chunky black sweater, the only thing I could do was pack her lunch, feed her breakfast, and drive her to school.

Thankfully, I didn't run into Clara in the hallway, and I didn't linger by the door with the hope that she would come out. Instead, I hugged Isabelle—despite her protests—and then hurried back to my car.

That's how I did every drop-off for the rest of the week.

Clara kept to herself. She spent the weekend after the play taking down all of her Christmas decorations until there was nothing left. I was grateful for her willingness to comply with the law here in Grinchland. It was nice that I didn't need to enforce anything.

I tried to ignore my broken heart as I watched her load up the moving truck the next weekend. I was standing off to the side with my coffee cup in hand, hoping she wouldn't notice that she had an audience. School was over, and it was time for winter break. I could only assume that meant she was headed back to Winter Springs to spend Christmas actually celebrating the holiday.

I told myself it was for the best. That she deserved to find someone who was equally as enthusiastic about Christmas as she was. I wanted to be that man for her, but I was only going to bring her down. I was never going to jeopardize my daughter's well-being for some twinkle lights and tinsel. And those were the things that made Clara happy.

I wasn't sure how long I stood there, watching Clara, but I stayed until the last box was loaded onto the moving truck and the back rolling door was shut and secured. I stayed long enough to see Clara glance up and down the street before her gaze lingered on my house, causing me to tuck myself further into the shadows so she wouldn't see me.

I stayed to watch her climb into her car and start the engine. And I stayed long after her car drove down the street and disappeared around the corner.

It was strange, Clara leaving. It was as if a light had been turned off both metaphorically and in actuality. I didn't want to admit it, but that woman had wiggled her way into my life whether I'd wanted her to or not. And now that she was gone...I felt her absence. More acutely than I'd thought I would.

Isabelle and I kept to ourselves during the first few days of winter break. We went to the ice rink a few times, and I stayed on land while she braved the ice herself. Her joy was contagious, and I couldn't help but smile as I watched her gain more confidence in her skating.

She hadn't brought up Clara since school got out, and I was beginning to feel as if our life was returning to normal until the morning of Christmas Eve. I walked into Isabelle's room to find her sitting on her floor with her dolls surrounding her. She was hard at work with her little tongue stuck out the corner of her mouth while she glued strips of paper for one of her doll's clothes.

Clothes that resembled something Clara would have worn.

She looked upset, so I moved to sit down next to her. "Everything okay, peanut?" I asked as I reached out to pick up the uneven star that she'd cut from yellow construction paper.

Isabelle glanced up at me, down to the star, and then back over to her doll. She was quiet for a moment. "Is Ms. Snow mad at me?"

I frowned and shook my head. "No. Ms. Snow isn't mad at you. Why would you think that?"

Isabelle glanced over to her window. "All the lights stopped and the sounds stopped." She looked up at me. "She's gone."

My heart broke for my daughter. It had to be hard, not understanding why people left you and yet being so acutely aware that they were gone. "She was just here to teach. She went back to her home for the break." I reached out and tugged her toward me, wrapping my arms around her tiny body.

"Oh." The word came out small and sad.

I bent forward and saw that her little bottom lip was jutted out, and it broke my heart. I hoisted her up into my lap so I could squeeze her tighter.

"I wish she would stay here forever."

I wanted to agree with her. I wanted to tell her that I wished for that too, but I could never make Clara happy. It was better to let her go and find her happiness somewhere else than to have her stay where the one thing she loved was forbidden.

Isabelle suddenly twisted in my lap so she could look up at me. "Is it because I messed up the play?"

Her voice wavered with sadness and it broke me inside.

I tucked her hair behind her ear before I shook my head. "No. She didn't leave because of you." She left because of me. I was the reason she wasn't here.

Isabelle's hands were turned palms up in her lap, and she was staring down at them. "I miss the colors. They made me feel happy."

I frowned as I shifted her up to sit on my left knee in an effort to catch her gaze. "Do you feel sad now?"

Isabelle's lip began to quiver as her gaze remained glued to her hands. "Ms. Snow made me feel excited. Since she left, I'm sad again." Finally, she raised her gaze to meet mine. "I don't want to feel sad again."

I stared at her, taking my daughter in. I searched her gaze for any sign of the apathy that I saw after the accident, but it wasn't there. Maybe Clara had been right. Maybe Isabelle just had a case of stage fright and I had overreacted. Isabelle was still with me. She was alive and breathing. Her eyes were bright, albeit sad.

And then guilt coated my chest.

In an effort to protect my daughter, I'd isolated her. I kept her from experiencing life because I was too scared that I would lose her. Instead of helping her live, she was slowly dying from my inability to see past my grief.

I'd taken things from my daughter with the hope that I was keeping her safe.

I thought canceling Christmas would make me feel

better, but in the last three years, I wasn't any happier. If anything, I was more unhappy than I'd ever been.

These last few weeks with Clara had made me happy, and I'd felt more free than I had in a long time. And Clara was the bringer of Christmas while I was the destroyer of it.

I stared at Isabelle, taking her all in and forcing myself to feel all of my emotions instead of running from them. I let myself feel sadness, grief, and anguish. But on the flip side, I also felt happiness, peace, and relief.

Just as all those emotions can exist in the same body, maybe Clara and I could exist in the same world as well. Sure we were opposites, but did that mean we weren't meant to be?

I helped Isabelle to stand and then stood myself. I walked over to her window and glanced out at Clara's quiet house. Tucked close to the garage was the tree that Isabelle had picked out.

I never thought I'd relate so closely to an inanimate object, but the longer I stared at it, the more I began to realize that I was like that tree. No one wanted me, but in Clara's hands, she had created something beautiful. Our little family was happier and brighter with her in it.

Christmas may have caused me pain in the past, but this year, it had brought a new beginning for Isabelle and me. And I was the idiot who let that new beginning pack up and drive away.

Isabelle was standing behind me, holding her dolls

tucked close to her chest and looking out the window. I turned and lifted her up. She giggled as she stared down at me.

"What do you think about going to get Ms. Snow?" I asked.

A smile emerged on her lips, and that was all I needed. I set her back down and instructed her to get her shoes on as I pulled my phone from my back pocket. I found my text chain with Todd and began to type.

> Call me ASAP. I need your help.

TWENTY-FIVE
CLARA

I'd never had such appreciation for my couch as I did in this moment. It was Christmas Eve, and instead of slaving away in front of the oven, making honey-glazed ham and the fluffiest mashed potatoes, I was lying on my couch in a cocoon of blankets, trying to get some sleep. But Abbie wasn't having it.

She was tapping her chin while pacing in front of me. "What about caroling?" She paused and pointed at me. "You love a good harmonization." She cleared her throat and hummed a few notes.

I pulled my blanket tight to my chin. "No," I said.

"Christmas cookies. And I promise this time I will try to decorate better."

I yawned. "I'm tired of Christmas cookies." That was a sentence I never thought I would say, and it almost felt criminal.

Abbie stared at me. It must have shocked her too. It took a moment for her to return to earth. She shook her head before she pointed at me again. "I've got it, last-minute presents. You *love* shopping for last-minute presents."

I shook my head. "No."

Abbie tossed her arms into the air before she let them fall to her sides. "Then what do you want to do?"

I snuggled deeper into the couch. "Sit here in my pajamas and veg."

Abbie glared at me before she swept her gaze over my body. "Those aren't even Christmas pajamas." She stepped up next to me and pressed her hand to my forehead.

I wiggled underneath her touch. "What are you doing?"

"Seeing if you're sick."

I stilled to appease her, and a few seconds later, she pulled her hand away.

"I'm writing that mayor a letter."

At the mention of Silas, my ears perked up. "What? Why?"

Abbie pulled her phone out of her back pocket. "I wanted you to detox a bit from your Christmas craziness, but he broke you. He needs to know that I'm not happy." She slid her finger on her screen like she was searching for something.

"Abbie, no," I said as I tried to find the opening to my

blankets so I could reach for her. "I just don't want to do anything today. There's no cause for alarm."

"Ha!" Abbie glanced over at me with her eyes wide. "And you don't see how that's not a problem?" She shook her head. "I'm leaving a review on Grinchland, and it is *not* going to be a positive one."

I gave up trying to unearth myself from the blankets and pillows and flopped back on the couch. I blew out my breath, knowing that when Abbie landed on a decision, there was nothing I could do to stop her.

She was fervently typing on her phone screen when there was a knock on the door. My stomach growled when I realized who it was.

"My Chinese," I said as I attempted to emerge from the layers of blankets. But when it became apparent that would be impossible, I glanced over to Abbie. "Be a dear and grab it for me?" I batted my eyelashes a few times in the hopes that would convince her.

Abbie narrowed her eyes before she turned and headed toward the front door. I waited until I heard the familiar squeak of the hinges and settled back in my lair.

"Can I help you?"

That seemed like a strange greeting to give a food delivery driver. I tipped my head to the side so my ear had full access to the conversation that was taking place twenty feet away.

"Is, um..." A man with a deep voice cleared his throat. "Is Clara here?"

My entire body both froze and flushed with heat at the same time. I blinked as I attempted to process whose voice I was hearing. It sounded like Silas, but that wasn't possible. He loved Grinchland and the tyranny he enacted there; he'd never leave.

"Is Clara here? Is *Clara* here?" she asked, her voice getting progressively louder as if she were trying to signal something to me. Whoever was at the door, Abbie felt I needed to be warned.

Could it really be Silas?

He must have been confused by Abbie's outburst because it took a moment for him to respond.

"Well, is she?"

I didn't want to leave my best friend in the lurch. I forced myself to roll off the couch and then wiggled out of the blanket cocoon. I stood, wiped the bottom of my eyes to try to look more alive, and then headed toward the front door.

"It's not Silas," I whispered to myself. I had imagined his voice, that was all.

Just as I rounded the corner, I straightened my shoulders and put on a smile to greet the delivery driver, but when my gaze landed on the figures standing there, my body went numb.

Isabelle and Silas were standing at my front door. Isabelle's eyes were wide as she looked all over my entryway. Silas looked irritated at Abbie as he waited for her to respond.

"Isabelle?" I asked before I could stop myself.

Isabelle's gaze landed on me, and before I could think, she sprinted over to me, wrapping her arms around my waist and squeezing hard. "Ms. Snow," she said, her voice muffled by my pajama top.

I instantly hugged her back, my heart aching for all the pain this little girl had gone through, including the pain I feared I'd inflicted on her by forcing Christmas on the town. "You're okay," I whispered as I crouched down so I could give her a once-over.

"I missed you," she said, her voice hushed as she leaned in closer to me.

I smiled back at her. "I missed you so much." I pulled her in for another hug.

"Guess what." She pulled back to look up at me.

I blinked back the tears that had formed on my eyelids. "What?" I said, matching the excitement in her voice.

"Christmas didn't kill me," she said matter-of-factly.

I raised my eyebrows. "Christmas didn't kill you?" I repeated back.

She shook her head. "It didn't. I'm okay. And I get to go to Catalina's party!"

My smile widened. "I'm so happy for you."

She nodded.

"We're working on reframing things. We're realizing that a holiday can't actually hurt us." Silas's voice grew nearer, and I wanted to look up at him. I wanted to see him again and get lost in his gaze. But I feared that once I allowed that connection, I was never going to be able to move on from him. I wasn't looking at him, but I could feel him. From the corner of my eyes, I could see him staring down at me.

"Your house is beautiful," Isabelle whispered as she glanced around, her gaze lingering on the living room.

"Thanks," I said. "Although, I'm thinking about clearing some of this stuff out and moving forward. After all, I need to stop living in the past."

That comment was more for Silas than Isabelle, but I still couldn't bring myself to look at him.

"Hey, Belly. Think you can give Ms. Snow and me a minute alone?"

Silas squatted down next to Isabelle, and my plan of never looking at him flew out the window. He was eye level to me now, and in my stupidity, I snapped my gaze over to him. He didn't meet my gaze. Instead, he just kept looking at his daughter.

"Why don't you come with me, and I'll show you Ms. Snow's snow globe collection. They are amazing," Abbie said as she stepped forward and reached out her hand.

Isabelle didn't need to be asked twice. She fervently nodded and slipped her hand into Abbie's, who then led her out of the foyer, leaving Silas and me alone.

Crouching there in silence, I knew I couldn't ignore that he was right in front of me, so I sighed and straightened. Silas moved to join me.

"So, is everything better in Grinchland now that

Christmas has officially been chased off?" I asked, not trying to hide the bite in my tone. I kept my gaze on the floor before I finally gathered my strength and turned to face him head-on.

Silas didn't respond right away. Instead, he just stood there, studying me.

"Isabelle misses you," he said as he shifted his weight and shoved his hands into the front pockets of his jeans.

"Isabelle misses me?" I repeated.

He nodded and then paused before he took a breath. "I miss you, too."

I frowned at him. "Because I was such an annoyance that now that I'm gone, you're bored?" I folded my arms across my chest. I wanted to believe that he meant what he said, but Silas had broken my heart, I wasn't ready to hand it to him again.

Silas studied me before he scoffed. "Clara," he whispered.

The soft way he said my name sent shivers across my skin. I wanted to lean into it. I wanted to close my eyes and jump headfirst into the feelings coursing through me, but I couldn't. Not when he could so quickly throw away the feelings that I knew he had for me.

"What?" I asked, trying to remain strong but failing miserably.

He glanced at the floor and then back up to me. "I was wrong," he said, shrugging his shoulders slightly.

I needed him to keep talking. I needed to hear everything. "About what?" I asked.

"A lot of things." He paused. "I was wrong about pushing away things that brought me joy. I was wrong to think that the best way to keep Nicole's memory alive was to slowly die myself." He swallowed, his jaw muscles flinching in the process. "I didn't want to hurt, so I hurt my daughter instead."

Emotions coated his voice, so he stopped to clear his throat. "Please come back. Isabelle and I need a little of your Christmas spirit in our lives. She—*I need you.*" He paused. "I want you."

A tear slipped down my cheek as I stared at him. I let go of all of my fear, all of my pain, and I closed the gap between us. Just as I neared him, I grabbed ahold of his jacket and yanked him to me, crashing my lips into his.

He didn't wait to respond, his hands finding my waist and pulling me to him until I wasn't sure where my body ended and his began.

His lips moved over mine, confirming to me what I'd suspected all along—*we were meant to be.*

A loud cheer came from the living room. Silas and I pulled apart, glancing over to see Isabelle standing on my couch, pumping her arms in the air. My face flushed as I glanced down at the floor, grateful that this little girl was as excited as I was.

"Belly, get off the couch like that," Silas scolded her but kept his arm wrapped tightly around my waist.

"Is Ms. Snow coming back with us?" Isabelle asked as she obediently climbed off the couch.

"It depends on if she wants to come back with us." He glanced over at me.

"Do you want to come back to live with me?" Isabelle asked as she skipped over to where we stood.

I glanced at Isabelle and then over to Silas. His gaze was so open and unabashed that it took my breath away.

"I would like that," I whispered, my emotions getting the best of me.

Silas leaned in and kissed me once more. "Merry Christmas, Clara," he murmured as he broke the kiss but kept his forehead touching mine.

I smiled, knowing what those words really meant. I pulled back slightly so I could meet his gaze. I wanted him to feel the power behind my words.

"I love you, too."

EPILOGUE

Silas

I might have made a mistake introducing Isabelle to Christmas. Once Clara told her about Santa, Isabelle was insistent that we bake cookies that night and put them out with a cold glass of milk.

Then, at five in the morning on the dot, Isabelle was in my bed, bouncing around to wake me up. It was time to see if Santa left her presents under the tree.

I had half a mind to declare that Christmas was re-banned just so I could get some more sleep, but I decided against it when I saw her wide eyes and flushed cheeks. Isabelle was meant for Christmas, and Christmas was meant for Isabelle.

Clara was sleeping on the couch when we walked into the living room. I grinned at her as she sat up and stretched. We figured that until we had things nailed down between us, it was best if we had boundaries when we were with Isabelle.

Luckily, Clara was Mrs. Claus and had been able to produce numerous presents for Isabelle at a moment's notice. So while Isabelle was busy ripping into the gifts, I snuggled with Clara on the couch, watching with a huge smile at the joy my daughter was experiencing. I had my arm wrapped tightly around her shoulders as I held her close to me.

Every so often, I leaned over and pressed my lips to her temple and whispered, "Merry Christmas," over and over again. She just smiled and tucked herself in closer.

We spent the afternoon ice skating and having a snowball fight. As seven o'clock neared, I ushered the two of them into the living room and told them to get ready.

Isabelle was bursting at the seams to tell Clara what we were doing, but I just pressed my forefinger to my lips and prayed that she could keep quiet. We had a surprise for Clara, and I wanted to see her reaction when we pulled into town square at seven-thirty on the dot.

I will never forget the gasp that came from Clara when I turned down Main Street. Her eyes were wide as she looked over at me. I couldn't stop grinning. My chest felt like it was going to explode.

"You didn't," she whispered as I pulled into my parking spot and turned off the engine. "Is that—"

"It's our tree!" Isabelle cheered. She was already

unbuckled and was climbing onto the center console between us.

Clara glanced over at Isabelle. "It is!"

"Come on, there's more," Isabelle said. The sound of her door opening had Clara and I reaching for our own door handles.

Clara's eyes were wide as she took in the sight. Todd had really pulled off something amazing. As soon as I told him my plan and that I was repealing the ban, he told me he'd take care of everything. The sheer number of decorations that started popping up around town shocked me. I had no idea that the man working next to me for so many years was such a massive Christmas fan.

He did an amazing job. The town looked so...festive. And the fact that Clara liked it made me love it even more.

"We're ready," Todd appeared next to me. I glanced over to see him standing next to our tree, which I'd brought to his house, telling him to make it the centerpiece of town square. It was covered in strings of lights and every branch held an ornament. Todd would never cease to amaze me.

I raised my eyebrows as I nodded toward the decorations. "The whole time?"

He shrugged. "What can I say?"

Regret coated my chest. "I'm sorry I forced you to hide it all."

He chuckled. "I knew you'd come to your senses eventually." Then he stepped closer to me. "For what you asked me about, I was able to find this." He held out his hand, and nestled in his palm was a gingerbread Christmas tree ornament. "Unfortunately, they don't make brown, dying Christmas tree ornaments. This was the best I could do."

I took it from him. "This will work." I glanced up. "Thanks."

He nodded. "Of course. And when you're done, the tree is ready to be lit."

"Perfect."

It didn't take me long to find Clara. She was laughing and talking to a group of townspeople who were all thanking her for bringing Christmas back. Their conversation hushed as I pushed through the group and wrapped my arm around her waist.

"I'm stealing you away," I murmured into her hair.

She giggled and followed me.

When we were a good distance away, I held out the ornament Todd had found for me. Clara studied it and then glanced up at me.

"What is this?" she asked.

"An ornament. So you can start collecting our memories."

She knit her eyebrows together for a moment before her lips made an "o" like she'd just realized what I was doing. "Because of the tree?" she asked, nodding in its direction.

"Isabelle's tree." I shrugged. "Apparently, they don't

make brown and dying tree ornaments, so this was the next best thing." I studied her. "Do you like it?"

She gently took the ornament out of my hand and held it up. She turned it a few times before her gaze met mine and I could see the tears brim on her eyelids. "I love it." She paused. "And I love you."

I didn't wait. I scooped her up into my arms and pressed my lips to hers. Gentle at first and then more fervently. Suddenly, someone cleared their throat and we pulled away.

"Come on you two turtle doves. There's no mistletoe around here. You've got a whole town waiting for you." Todd smiled at us.

I stepped back and Clara did the same. I didn't let her go too far as I grabbed ahold of her hand and walked toward the tree where the town had gathered. I wanted to just plug the Christmas lights in and have that be the end of the event, but people began to chant, "Speech!" and Clara looked expectantly over to me, so I decided to give them what they wanted.

I started out saying I was grateful that the people of Grinchland had understood that I was struggling. I told them that I'd never felt more loved or cared for. And then I apologized for canceling Christmas in the first place.

"From here on, Grinchland will now celebrate Christmas—" I boomed, and the entire crowd began to cheer. Clara louder than anyone else.

I raised my forefinger, and the celebration grew quiet.

Once I had everyone's attention, I finished the rest of that sentence. "Grinchland will now celebrate Christmas... within reason."

With that, I grabbed the plug, stuck it into the outlet, and the lights on the tree gleamed.

***

If you're wanting more between Silas and Clara, check out their SWEET Bonus scene below.

Enjoy!
Grinchland SWEET scene: HERE or scan below

Want more of Christmas from Anne-Marie Meyer? Check out her Christmas Romance Bundle. Head on over and grab it HERE.

Want more from Anne-Marie Meyer?
Try the Red Stiletto Bookclub.
Head on over and grab your next read HERE.

For a full reading order of Anne-Marie's books, you can find them HERE.
Or scan below:

Made in United States
Orlando, FL
01 November 2025